Frontier Wanderer

By

Alberto Büchi

Alberto Büchi

Published By: Siento Sordida,
an Imprint of Caliburn Press, LLC.
Originally accepted by Eternal Press,
an Imprint of Caliburn Press, LLC
P.O. Box 8747
Madison, WI 53714
Frontier Wanderer by Alberto Büchi
Translated by Sarah Silver
Cover art by: Cinsearae Santiago
Edited by: Sally Odgers

Digital ISBN: 978-1-62929-350-9
Print ISBN: 978-1-62929-351-6
ISBN 10: 1629293504

DEDICATION

To my everlasting love, my little dog Toffee.

ACKNOWLEDGMENTS

Thanks to:
My family first of all, for their patience and support;
Sarah Silver and Jo Macfarlane for the great job;
Paul Edwin Zimmer with the trilogy of the Lost Prince and
Nicolas Winding Refn with Valhalla Rising for the
inspiration;
Romero and all the "Zombie culture";
Mario Arturo Iannacone, Paolo Restuccia and Enrico Valenzi
for their advices and guidance;
Linda Pesce and Fabiano Exana because life is full of
coincidences;
Gippo Salvetti for his friendship and support;
Chiara Bennici for the extraordinary patience;
... and those who have already read the book and those who
will read it.

Chapter One

The powerful black stallion advanced slowly across the ravine. Breath burst from the horse's nostrils, condensing on contact with the cold air. The threadbare leather trappings were rough, sodden, and hardened by the elements.

Hansio had wrapped a gray fur over his shoulders and tied it around his neck. Despite the fact his hands were covered in tiny sores from the cold, he still managed to maintain a tight grip on the reins. His face was drawn and angular, his build thin yet imposing. He had long, brown, dreadlocked hair and a beard that trailed down to his chest.

The man, known as 'The Hero of the Dying Lands', lifted his gaze to the mountain peaks in the distance, the ones that were not obscured by the clouds. He looked for the sun and found it cold and gray, rising behind a summit in the east. As he proceeded, the dense, white fog coated his beard in tiny beads of ice. Behind them, at just a dozen or so paces, a man followed on the brink of hypothermia. A metal ring hung painfully around his neck and a rope secured him to the stallion's saddle. His hands were tied, his clothes caked with blood and earth. Suddenly, he tripped and fell heavily to the ground. Hansio, acknowledgement barely flashing through his ferocious yellow eyes, moved on with his horse and the rope tightened, dragging the man through the mud. The prisoner managed to get back on his feet and continued walking.

They arrived in a boggy area of the gorge and the Hero dismounted, his feet sinking deep into the soggy, lifeless ground. The horse's hooves sank even farther than the feet of the warrior, who looked around him, scowling. The rocky walls of the ravine were steep and strewn with ice-shattered rocks and feeble, sporadic clumps of vegetation. The freezing wind grew stronger, piercing their skin like needles of ice.

Hansio realized his prisoner would have trouble keeping up and tugged on the rope harshly. Even though the strength had almost left him and he had trouble keeping his head up, the man took the blow without falling. The warrior seized the reins of the horse and moved forward until they reached a tree trunk that penetrated deep into the ground.

Hansio caressed the horse's nose, then untied the rope and pulled the man towards him, this time more gently. He took a water sack from the horse's saddle and passed it to the man, who seemed oblivious to the sudden gesture of compassion. Hansio quickly stepped forward and slapped his forehead with the palm of his hand. The prisoner lifted his chin, saw the water and took it clumsily, his fingers fumbling. His bound hands were too numb and swollen to hold anything, even something light, and the sack slipped to the ground. Irritated, Hansio picked it up impatiently. Grabbing the prisoner by the hair, he pulled his head back until his mouth gaped open, pouring the water down his throat as best he could, making the man cough and splutter. The soft sack made it difficult to pour and the water gushed all over his face.

He let go of the prisoner's hair and pushed his head to one side, making him sway. He then untied his hands, put the sack back on the saddle and turned towards the tree trunk. The prisoner, who had been watching him closely, now realized his intentions.

"Wh...what are you doing?" slurred the prisoner, another cough racking his body.

Hansio gave no answer and continued to fasten the rope despite the wind that blew his hair in front of his face. The two small braids that hung in front of his ears managed to resist the weaker gusts of wind.

"Why are you tying me to this post?" the man struggled to speak, the muscles of his face stiffened by the cold.

Hansio pulled the man towards him and fixed his yellow eyes on him with a malicious scowl.

The prisoner wailed and threw himself upon the ground and, as if he had managed to reserve some energy for his pleas, gripped the Hero's clothes like a desperate beggar.

"Please, don't hurt me! Let me go! Is this why you freed me, so you could torture me?"

The Hero took a knife from his belt and abruptly slashed the man's arm. Blood splattered across his beard and lips. The prisoner howled and fell into the mud, nursing his injured limb. An echo of the man's tortured cries was heard in the distance and the deep red blood mingled with the wet earth. Hansio licked his blood-flecked lips, stooped over the man and cut him again, slicing his chest open.

"Why are you doing this to me? Why?" his victim sobbed. Despite the shallow wounds, the blood flowed in abundance. Hansio said nothing. The warrior put his weapon back in its sheath, ripped off some shreds from the man's blood-soaked clothes and turned his back on the prisoner. He grabbed the reins of the stallion and the beast huffed, creating a cloud of vapor.

* * * *

"No, not this, I beg you..." the man said between sobs. "You can't leave me here. We are at least two leagues beyond the Frontier. We are in the Infested Lands..." he sank his head into the bloody mud as if begging for mercy.

"It's full of the living dead here—they'll smell my blood. Please don't do this to me! They'll be here soon, looking for food...the blood will attract them by the dozen!" his tears mingled with the drool pooling from his mouth.

Hansio ignored his pitiful cries and led his horse onwards.

"I don't want to die like this...this is inhumane. Why do you condemn me to this soulless death?"

'Soulless'. The words echoed in the Hero's head, stopping

him in his tracks.

"Please, come back! Cut my throat if you must, but don't let me be eaten alive. I don't want to become one of them!"

Without looking back, Hansio continued on his way, the wind behind him. His tiny braids swayed in the breeze.

"I beg you! Don't leave me to those beasts! In the name of the gods!"

Hansio could hold back no longer. He dropped the reins and turned around furiously. He paced over to the wretched man and lifted him up by his neck. Hansio's teeth ground together and he let out an angry cry.

"The gods do not exist!" Hansio hissed, in a leaden and emotionless reply to the man's pleas.

He threw the man against the tree trunk and punched him violently in the face. He held back the true extent of his rage. If he broke his face he would kill him before the time had come.

"You were in a cage when I found you," Hansio roared. "They would have chopped off your head with an axe. You were a dead man anyway. Here or in that fetid town where I found you—it makes no difference. Your death will be worthwhile for the 'cull' I must do."

He grabbed him by the hair so he could look him in the face. "There is no god to save your soul! I doubt that either of them exists anyway. The Hastur are wrong. Look up there!" he pointed to the sky, roughly pushing his face to make him look. "The sun is dying. That is the true symbol of our soulless lives."

After setting the man down, Hansio systematically spread strips of blood-soaked cloth within a radius of a hundred paces from the post, then others slightly further away. He took the horse away from the boggy ravine and set up camp on some nearby rocks. He was in an elevated position, where he could keep an eye on what was soon to come. He was certain, because he had already used this place in his many travels beyond the Frontier. It might have been a desert of rocks and ice, but the walking dead could be found everywhere. They were here too, and just like fish they would take his bait of meat and blood.

With the stallion well under cover, the Hero lit a small fire. The thin flames illuminated his sword, which he had carefully placed beside him. It was as long as his leg, maybe even more. The pommel was in the shape of a half-moon and was engraved with words from the sacred language of the Hastur. The same marks were also on the cross-shaped guard and etched inside the grooves of the blade. Hansio stared at it, as he often did, disgusted by what it represented with its magic and its origins. His contempt also stemmed from the fact he had never been able to free himself of it. Something in his conscience prevented him and he found this too much to bear.

I must cleanse this land, he thought , trying to crush his anxiety.

He bit into an apple, ate half and gave the rest to his horse. Then he turned his gaze towards the tree trunk where the man was tied up and stood there staring back at him.

Come on little fish. Come and take the bait. Make my task easier, come here all of you, he thought.

All around the clouds clung to the earth and rocks, as if struggling to reach the sky, thinning out and dispersing as soon as they gained altitude. He decided he could afford to take a rest.

There was no need to keep an eye on the bait, because he would not be able to run away. In any case, the arrival of the living dead would be announced by the man's screams. Furthermore, his position provided the horse with a good hiding place.

Still wrapped in his furs, he closed his eyes.

* * * *

As he foresaw, he was awoken by the cries of the unfortunate prisoner. He looked at his sword and knew it was time, because it emitted a glowing blue light. He stood up and saw the typical swaggering gait of the living dead in the distance. He watched as the lure tried to run, but was stopped by the rope. The backlash made him fall in the mud. It reminded Hansio of a dog that was too stupid to realize it was tied up. If he carried on like that he would break his neck. Gripped with terror, the captive tried to pull on the rope. Hansio smiled.

The living dead were close by, but intervening now would be foolish. The whole idea of the bait was to attract as many prey as possible.

The Hero scrutinized the two entrances into the ravine, but did not see any other silhouettes in the distance. He decided to wait, observing the scene as the living dead fed upon the fresh flesh of the wretch.

The scene disgusted him, making his stomach churn with so much rage that when he would finally leap upon his prey to break their skulls, the satisfaction would be immense. It would be a release, a liberation. Hacking off the heads of those beings and seeing their rotten brains would give him a pleasure that was almost sexual.

* * * *

The blue light of the Hastur sword grew increasingly more intense.

One of the living dead now closed in on the human lure and the desperate cries were harrowing. The man tried to flee, but could do nothing more than run aimlessly, prolonging his agonizing terror. The boggy ground made it hard for him to move and he slipped. He got to his feet again and tugged on the rope, but it would not give.

Meanwhile, Hansio had not realized there were now two

living dead and others were joining them.

Deranged with terror, once again, the prey tried to escape but fell into the mud. One of the dead was immediately upon him.

A familiar squirt of blood flew upwards and Hansio thought the creature must have ruptured one of the man's arteries. The second sank its teeth into his leg. A third and then a fourth soon arrived to share the remains. Hansio was so inflamed he could no longer hear the prisoner's screams. The bait always screamed in the same way. Once you had heard one, you had heard them all. When the Hero decided to intervene the man had already stopped struggling and screaming. Hansio gripped his glowing sword and came out from his hiding place. After a few steps, he looked back at his horse then continued on his way. There was no point running because the living dead were now bent over the bait and, driven by hunger as they were, would certainly not abandon the body. However, the ones who had not yet had their fill would soon pick up his scent and come for him. When the first of the creatures was within sword's reach, Hansio struck his first cleaving blow—the angriest one— slicing the living dead in half from head to ribcage. The blade was so sharp it could have cut through rock.

A foul, suffocating stench of cadaver rose into the air.

The inhuman sounds that came from the beings' mouths, halfway between a grunt and a snarl, compelled him to act even more ferociously.

Soon Hansio confronted five of them all at the same time. They were dim-witted, but could always rely on their numbers. If he had been unlucky enough to trip or lose his weapon, he could have fought back the first with his fists, but he would soon be overpowered by the bites of the others. The blade let out an intense blue glare, rising and falling, hacking off hands and heads.

Hansio got immense pleasure from splitting their heads in two or slashing them horizontally at eye level, exposing their craniums. He had seen many of their rotten brains this way. Suddenly he found himself surrounded by more of them. There was no longer any room to move his sword. This was one of the risks he knew he might come up against.

He pierced one with his sword to slow them down, but its hands reached for his neck, its teeth gnashing together with a disturbing sound. It was impaled from one side to the other, but the cadaver continued to close in on him, preventing him from extracting his sword.

Suddenly Hansio felt a hand on his shoulder.

Leaving his sword where it was, he moved with agility and speed, pushing the creature in front of him back. He turned suddenly and shoved the new aggressor away with the sole of his foot. The creature fell onto the other two, slowing down their progress. It was only in that instant he realized what a risk he took. The creature was so close he smelled the stench of its breath.

Hansio turned to pick up his sword but, before he had time to think, another lurched towards him and they fell together into the mud. Instinctively he grabbed the creature by its neck to keep its jaws away from his flesh. They were trying to grab and scratch him with their blue-gray, broken nails. Hansio squeezed the creature's neck so tightly he felt something snap beneath his fingers. He had to move fast, because soon the other ravenous beings would be upon him. With a cry of rage, he freed one of his hands and pulled his knife from his belt. He felt more of them gripping his ankle. He kicked out sharply and one of them fell backwards. Summoning up all his power, he rammed the short blade into the eye of the being on top of him. It immediately slumped. He pulled out his knife and got back on his feet, just in time to slash another that was coming towards him.

The blade sliced off part of its nose and poked out an eye, but was not enough to kill it, because the weapon had not pierced the brain. Hansio adjusted his grip and stabbed the knife forcefully into its forehead.

Losing his knife in the creature's skull meant he now had to recover his sword quickly.

He caught a glimpse of a blue glare and reached for it, still impaled inside the body of the creature he fought earlier. He packed a couple of punches and picked up a stone, which he used to split open the head of the nearest creature, then threw it at the one pierced by his blue blade. He hit it directly in the mouth, knocking out a few teeth. Then he reached out a hand, grabbed the hilt and freed the sword. He turned and struck the creature behind him directly on the head. With his weapon back in his hands, he now finished off the rest of them without too much interference.

* * * *

Hansio raised his sword for the umpteenth time, gripping the hilt with both hands, and suddenly realized his enemies were finished. He was panting and enormous white clouds of breath bellowed from his mouth. His body was so hot, it fumed in the cold air. He was immediately satisfied by the massacre. At least thirty mutilated bodies lay in the mud. He lowered his sword and took a deep breath. The smell of the putrefied flesh was so strong it made his head spin and, as always, he felt the need for purification.

He could not see any others in the distance, so he decided to burn everything he had slashed to pieces.

Close by were the remains of a large funeral pyre he used some time ago. He piled the bodies and dismembered limbs on top of it and used a flame from the fire he had lit earlier to light it. It took a long time before the flames were high enough to carbonize the mass of rotten flesh.

He left what remained of the human lure in the mud. The

man still had the rope around his neck but one of his cheeks had been completely stripped of flesh. An arm had been ripped off and lay a few meters away, completely consumed. The same fate had almost befallen a leg, which was partially detached from his hip. The head was still firmly attached to the body, which meant sooner or later those remains would reawaken, incapable of movement, but still hungry for blood. Hansio retrieved his sword, the blue glow now almost diminished, and drove it into the man's neck. He grabbed the head by the hair and threw it to the pyre.

That was the only gesture of pity the Hero of the Dying Lands could muster.

Chapter Two

The Frontier was on the other side of the woods Hansio crossed. Most of the trees and shrubs were dead and the pathway was scattered with numerous pieces of dry wood. The low branches prevented him from riding. He was forced to proceed on foot, leading the stallion by the reins. The shadow of the woods made the air damp and consequently the cold felt more acute.

Hansio was tired, and a sense of emptiness in his chest made him stop in a spot where the light struggled to filter through. He grabbed his water sack and took a large swig. His weak body clouded his mind and distressing thoughts took over. He tied the stallion to a broken tree trunk and tried to overcome the sense of claustrophobic anxiety that welled up inside. He looked for the gray sky and found it between some branches of the spectral woods.

The sight of the dying sun comforted him, because in it he saw the confirmation that everything would come to an end—life, the exhausting battle with the living dead, and the emptiness inside of him. The end comforted him every time his legs grew weak and whenever he became disgusted with life. He clenched his fists, his knuckles turning white.

Suddenly, a thud a short distance away put him on alert. Being close to the Frontier did not mean you were safe from the living dead. In fact, his sword began to glow blue and the anger that built up inside him helped him find some strength, shutting away his thoughts. Another rustle helped him work out the direction of the sound. Hansio drew his sword, moving silently, clenching it in his fist. After a dozen or so steps, behind a tree with a large trunk, he saw a woman with disheveled hair with her back towards him.

The waft of rotten flesh was unmistakable, as was the sound of teeth slicing into bones.

The woman was stooped over a pile of red sludge, bones and hairs that writhed with white maggots. Judging by the long ears, Hansio realized it was the remains of a hare that had probably died of hunger. The carcass of the mammal surprised him more than the presence of the woman. In the Dying Lands wild animals were rare and even more so beyond the Frontier, where the infestation of the living dead rendered the water putrid, the air unbreathable and the land sterile. The more you moved away from the Dying Lands, the more the life of humans and animals became impossible. Furthermore, the animals could smell death and would instinctively flee.

Hansio observed what had once been a woman, as it fed upon the fleshless remains.

His was a morbid fascination that compelled him to study them. He stood in wait behind the tree, wondering if she still had a sense of taste and touch, if thoughts still lived inside her rotten brain. Smell was the only sense he was certain they still possessed. He even wondered what they felt when they ate human flesh.

No divine being could bear a similar end for their offspring, he thought. He always arrived at the same conclusion.

Hansio made no other sound than his own breathing, but the woman soon became aware of his presence. She suddenly stopped eating, sniffed the air and turned towards him.

The Hero presumed she had been transformed only recently, because her clothes were still intact, apart from a tear on one of her hips, where her body had been partially devoured. A piece of intestine poked out of her abdomen. With a shred of fur still hanging from her mouth, the dead woman stood up awkwardly and growled.

Her skin was gray and shriveled in places and she had purple circles under her eyes. The lips were the same color, but slightly paler. Like all the walking dead, it seemed as if her red-rimmed eyes were bleeding. Her pupils were so dilated they looked like the dark depths of a well. She had rotten teeth and a black tongue. The being advanced towards the Hero, who stood immobile. The fur fell from her mouth to the ground with a gentle thud.

Hansio raised his sword and split her head open with a measured and efficient blow. The creature fell instantly to the ground and the sword slowly turned back to the color of metal.

Despite this sudden show of strength and agility, tiredness still ailed his limbs and the emptiness inside him remained. The woman fell with what little was left of her face pressed against the earth. Hansio turned her over with his foot, but then felt the need to sit down, overwhelmed with fatigue. He leaned against a rise of earth and then his thoughts returned to his horse. There were probably other living dead nearby, because the inhabitants of the villages near the Frontier were often attacked and killed by their random incursions or by friends or family who had just been transformed. It was also for this reason that the frontier receded, continually eroded by the incessant proliferation of death. He spotted the stallion, standing calmly beyond some trees. His blade did not warn of any unnatural presences, so he was happy to rest a while. He dug the point of his sword into the ground, gripped the hilt and leaned his head on his hands. The stench was unbearable and the air almost impossible to breathe, but he needed to let that moment of prostration pass before continuing on his path.

He sat there motionless for a while then lifted his gaze, observing the scene before him. The decomposing hare seemed less repulsive than the corpse of the dead woman, even though her body looked almost intact from where he stood. Maybe it was due to the clothes she wore.

Suddenly he heard another rustle and immediately thought

another living dead had picked up his scent.

The Hastur sword did not alert him of a presence. Hansio jumped to his feet, scrutinizing the trees, but there were no movements, other than the black stallion. He was certain his horse had not made that noise.

The atmosphere had changed as if reality altered somehow. A cold wind whistled through the branches, bringing with it something strange. It was disturbing and mysterious, even though Hansio could not explain why. It was as if it came from far away. He raised his sword and stood on guard. His warrior instinct told him something was happening and he needed to defend himself. Suddenly, he realized a thick, white fog–which appeared from nowhere–covered his feet, swallowing up the body of the woman and the hare. Then another, more violent gust of wind arrived, but did not carry the mist away.

Hansio stepped forward, his sword ready to parry any sudden blow. His hands gripped the hilt tightly but no light came from the blade. So why were his instincts telling him to be on guard? He looked around, his yellow eyes intent on catching any movement, his ears at the ready to aid his reflexes.

The fog was now up to his knees, but it seemed to have stopped growing. The muscles of his arms and face tensed. The sound of hooves on the ground, close by, caused him to turn sharply. A warrior on a powerful horse stood before him, a warrior Hansio knew well.

Martos, from the Southern Lands, was surrounded by a blue aura, similar to the light of the Hastur sword. He possessed a similar weapon, which was now on the saddle in its sheath, and he too had penetrating yellow eyes.

He was a Hero of the Dying Lands. Hansio observed the warrior from head to foot, struck by the awe-inspiring vision before him. The other Hero carried a large double-headed axe, a sign of his strength and his favorite weapon before he acquired the Hastur sword.

"Hansio of the Gray Sea, lower your sword. You have nothing to fear from an equal, your ancient companion in arms."

Martos's voice was deeper than Hansio remembered and seemed to come from a distant place. It was exactly the same sensation he felt just before the wind that announced his appearance.

"What do you want from me?" his tone was one he would have used with an enemy.

"Far away from here, in this very moment, the life is leaving my body." Martos's yellow eyes flickered.

A red blotch appeared on his chest.

Hansio lowered his gaze, observing the Hero on horseback with different eyes.

He almost wished he could change places with Martos.

"The last memory I have of you was when..." Hansio hesitated, his voice breaking. "I can't stand the sight of you..."

"I can imagine how sad and painful that day was for you," Martos interrupted. "I understand how it is still an open wound for you even today."

"So, why do you think I would be concerned about what becomes of you?"

"Because I was struck while carrying out their will."

"I still don't understand why you came to me."

Martos explained. "The Hastur of the great soul—"

Hansio interrupted him angrily. "You have come here in vain. You risk my wrath! I have nothing in common with them. Go back to where you came!"

"Your insanity is so grave? I must remind you your vow still ties you to them! I always hoped the rumors of your wanderings beyond the Frontier, intent on a senseless hunt, were maybe exaggerations. In the same way I have never wanted to accept that you no longer believe in the soul, that you no longer accept the love of the gods."

"Gods and souls are the inventions of the useless beings you serve!" replied Hansio.

"The Hastur are illuminated by the light of the gods. Your insanity cannot have made you as blind as this. You speak such blasphemy!"

Hansio's words were bitter. "Shut up and die! Get out of my sight!"

With a sudden ferocious movement he lashed out, but his sword went straight through Martos and his horse, as if they were made of smoke. Prepared for the impact, the empty lunge knocked Hansio clumsily off balance.

Enshrouded in his blue halo, the other Hero spoke angrily. "I will die, this is certain, but I have come to warn you...finding you in this state, my soul will not be able to reach the gods without fearing the Dying Lands will come to an end before their time. We need Heroes to keep the Resistance alive until the Great Exodus, until the Hastur complete the Ark."

"I piss on your soul and the Ark! I have no need of your warnings."

"Then all hope will die with me...just when the Hastur have never been closer to completing the miracle."

Hansio watched as the red mark on Martos's chest grew bigger.

"It has been hundreds of years...maybe even more...maybe from when the sun first died that humanity has waited for the Hasturs' miracle."

Hansio was scornful yet something perplexed him. "What do you mean with you dies all hope? What is the true meaning of this visitation?"

"The Hasturs' powers have allowed me to communicate with you, to tell you that you are the last. The last Hero of the Dying Lands."

"The last?" Hansio's voice trembled.

"All the Heroes of the Dying Lands are now with the gods."

"How is this possible?"

"The living dead continue to grow in number and the Hooded Ones are breeding with our women. The sieges of the creatures bring us to the brink of exhaustion. Their fighting manner is sly and the more they kill the more numerous they become."

Hansio recovered his angry assertiveness. "The Frontier is receding continually. The Dying Lands grow smaller...our reality is destined to vanish into nothingness. I can do nothing to save you. No one can, this is the order of things. It must be accepted."

"Maybe you are right. The reality as we know it is destined to vanish. The sun is dying after all, but our existence will not vanish into nothingness. You too believed in the Ark once. The language of the gods is not easy to understand, but the Hastur are close to interpreting their instructions for the new lands."

"Falsehoods."

"Falsehoods or not, you are the last Hero and the responsibility of the Resistance now falls upon you. Your vow is still alive and you must use your Hastur sword far better than you have done with the living dead of the Frontier."

"I am no longer their servant."

"You are the servant of no one. The sword you hold is the symbol of your oath and only the Hastur or death can release you from it. Heed my words—you are the last Hero of these wretched lands."

"No!" shouted Hansio furiously. "I want to be in your place!"

"Hansio, the future is bleak. The Dying Lands need Heroes to protect them. I will die a sad man if you wish to be in my place."

"That is not possible...so die and leave me be."

"You will receive another call. This is the last beat of my heart. My time has come."

Hansio looked on as the blood stain spread out across his entire chest.

Martos pulled on the reins and turned his horse around without another word.

The mist was sucked back into the ground and, once more, Hansio found himself alone.

Chapter Three

The sun had already gone down by the time Hansio reached the first village beyond the Frontier. He had visited this place a long time ago and when he turned his back on it, he wondered if he would find it again within the Dying Lands. Even in those days, the inhabitants dwindled, some fleeing south, others devoured and transformed. The Frontier had retreated a lot since then.

In villages like these, there were many tales of fathers forced to kill their own children to prevent them waking from the dead, or vice versa. Hansio deeply hoped he would not have to hear another.

On the tattered outskirts of the village were a few abandoned stone houses. Their wooden roofs were swollen and deformed by damp or had collapsed. The shattered windows and broken-down doors were the tell-tale signs of passing looters or assaults by the living dead, who had smelt the fresh flesh of the houses' former occupants.

However, as far as he could tell, it appeared the inhabitants had managed to keep the resistance alive, because there were still signs of life in the village. Hansio wondered why they fought so long and hard, considering sooner or later the Infested Lands would swallow up everything. It was only a question of time.

Hansio trotted along on his horse. He felt uneasy and observed, as if someone spied on him from one of the dilapidated windows. His muscles were exhausted yet tense, his palm caressing the pommel of the Hastur sword. A living cadaver wandered somewhere, he knew, because the sword emanated a weak blue glow.

It's certainly not close, judging by the intensity of the blade, he thought.

Hansio turned and in the distance, behind some trees, he

thought he made out a shadow. He was tired and hungry and had reached the entrance to the village, so he decided to ignore it.

The horse's hooves passed from the waterlogged ground of the muddy road to the wood of the bridge that led to the village gate, making a dull thud in the silence.

The bridge passed over the bed of what had once been a brook, which originated from somewhere within the Infested Lands. All that remained now was a foul-smelling stream.

The inhabitants had built a barrier with tree trunks to protect themselves from the wandering dead. Under the light of two torches, a sentry was posted at the top of a tower. His crossbow leaned against the parapet.

"Open up!" cried Hansio to the guard. "I need food and a bed for the night."

Then, remembering himself, he added hastily, "I can pay or barter."

The guard thought for a moment, evaluating the situation, and then let out a whistle. The gates opened just enough to let Hansio through.

Gently spurring the black stallion on, he entered the village. He was met by two men, the first with a disfigured face, who immediately closed the gate behind him, and the second with a moronic gaze, who clutched a wood axe. Their bodies were protected only by thick pieces of leather.

It was astonishing, the Hero thought, that this village had become an outpost of the Resistance.

"Who are you, who does not fear traveling by night?" the disfigured man asked. "Are you a madman? Do you not know that the Infested Lands are only two leagues away?"

Hansio pretended not to hear.

"I remember an inn, is it still here?" the Hero asked. "Is there anywhere I can get any food?"

The disfigured man spat on the ground between the hooves

of the stallion and pointed to the village's main street.
Hansio directed his horse, vaguely remembering the way
from his previous visit. His yellow eyes remained fixed on his
sword, which still emanated a blue light.

An infected person might be in the village, he thought, or
maybe the sword glowed because this was a place where the
living dead flocked. Hansio was tired and needed to rest.

As long as I am not attacked, it doesn't concern me, he told
himself.

Still, Hansio resolved to keep an eye on his sword for the
entire duration of his stay. He would sleep with it beside
him.

The streets were deserted and few light s shone in the
dwellings.

As he neared the inn, he crossed paths with another young
guard. He was not wearing any chainmail and possessed only
a dagger and a dented helmet that was far too big for him.
Hansio doubted he would survive a clash with two living
dead at the same time. Maybe one—if he didn't let fear take
over.

The luminescent warning of the Hastur sword still showed
no signs of receding.

He passed over a light rise and reached the courtyard of the
inn. The door was above three steps, beneath a faded sign
with a picture of a red pig. The letters of the name were
eroded by time and neglect.

There was one lantern in the courtyard, but the light was
sufficient to illuminate a small area. Hansio tied his horse
and observed the two floors of the inn. The windows of the
room were dark and, with uncharacteristic irony, he thought
he would not have any trouble finding a bed for the night.

He took his leather bag from his horse and entered. The
room was dimly lit but warm. A large hearth guarded a small
fire and every table had its own candle stub. Only three were

lit, to allow the inn's few patrons to see their food in their wooden bowls. Hansio counted three tables and five people. Some of the customers were armed with daggers and axes, weapons useful for close combat. They were probably guards of the Resistance taking a break.

Would they have the ability and courage to look at one of the living dead up close and put up with its smell of death? Arrows were safer but archers needed to be skilled and agile. An old man wearing a white, grease-stained apron approached the Hero. His build was skinny, his demeanor nervous, and he carried a tray with three empty tankards. He eyed Hansio suspiciously.

"I need food, a bed and a safe stable for my horse," said Hansio.

The old man scrutinized the Hero, teasing a tooth with his tongue.

"I don't know you," the man said. "We don't get travelers around these parts, unless they are bringing a message from the Hastur, may the gods illuminate their minds!"

His tone was mistrustful but immediately became more cutting. "Wanderers, on the other hand, are not welcome."

Hansio was shocked by this angry outburst, but after so much time, all he desired was a hot meal. He was in no mood for a discussion.

He wanted to tell the old man the Hastur were the same 'great souls' asking poor devils, like those sitting in his inn, to fight against the living dead without adequate protection. This was in complete contrast to the great importance the Hastur placed on life. It was just another lie, along with all the other lies they preached to the wretched.

"I can pay," Hansio offered, dropping a jingling money bag onto a nearby table.

"I have no use for coins," the old man scoffed.

"What about these?" Hansio pulled a bundle of ten candles

from his sack. Some were partially used. The old man's eyes
sharpened and he raised an eyebrow.

Hansio noticed the man throwing furtive and avid glances at
his sack.

"Those will be enough for the food," the man conceded.
"Even for tomorrow if there are any leftovers."

Then he spotted a long mouthpiece poking out of Hansio's
bag. "What's that? A pipe?"

"Yes, but you can't have it."

"I'm not interested in your pipe, I'm interested in tobacco,"
the man insisted. "Have you got any?"

"Yes, I have."

The man smiled, revealing the yellow teeth of a lifelong
smoker.

"Very well, you can stay for tonight," the old man purred.
"You can use the stable on the other side of the courtyard."

Hansio knew he was paying much too high a price, but he let
it slide and went to put his stallion away safely for the night.
The stable was deserted but there was hay and it would keep
the animal safe from the attacks of the living dead. He
removed the trappings and caressed its nose. The horse was
agitated but his touch calmed him down. Hansio returned to
the inn and sat at an isolated table in the dark. He felt the
mistrustful gaze from other travelers. One of them belched
without breaking his stare.

Hansio did not want to attract attention, but a man of his
stature with so many objects to barter could not go
unnoticed. He avoided eye contact and covered his face with
his hair. He was no longer a Hero.

A plain-faced girl with generous breasts and broad hips came
out of the kitchen. Her hair was gathered at her neck and she
carried a tankard and a wooden bowl.

She placed both down heavily on Hansio's table. They
contained an off-white steaming slop and a dark liquid. A

few pieces of vegetables he did not recognize floated on the top.

To his surprise, he noticed it was hot.

He gestured to the girl that there was no need to light the candle. Hansio watched the woman return to the kitchen and when she had gone he grabbed the bowl in both hands.

The hot broth slipped down his throat, into his stomach, and he immediately felt the beneficial effects of its warmth. After the first few sips, he felt physically and psychologically restored. The cold in the Infested Lands was not the usual cold. It clung to your skin, penetrated your muscles and then the bone, and would lurk within you for a long time. The slop was old and burnt, but Hansio was used to eating worse. A drink from the tankard confirmed it contained watered-down wine.

The faded taste of the drink summoned a long-forgotten memory of a life that no longer belonged to him. These days, Hansio could hardly be sure it had ever existed.

He sat at a table with many people and before him was a plate laden with roast meat. They were in a castle, near a stormy sea, where the salt made the air pungent. He raised a glass of red wine to his lips. The robust taste was already on his tongue and in the chair next to him was…

He suddenly grabbed a hand stretched out before him. The girl had returned to take away the empty bowl. Without raising his head, Hansio said, "I have been here before…"

The feeble light cast disturbing shadows across his face.

"Really?" the woman looked at him fearfully.

"Yes. Back then, along with a bed for the night, they also offered something else…"

* * * *

Hansio gripped the girl's breast with such violence that her mouth dropped open. Her sharp cry of pain excited him all the more. He tore the upper part of her dress, exposing her pale breasts and sank his teeth into them. The girl desperately tried to fight him off but her weak fists were useless. Hansio pushed her violently towards the filthy bed, roughly turned her around and forced her to bend over. Lifting up her long skirt, he bent down to bite the back of her thigh. Paying no attention to her anguished cries, he bit her again and again, squeezing and scratching her. Then, he lifted her skirt once more and hurled it over her head.

"Please don't hurt me," the girl begged, as if regretting what she had agreed to do.

She turned her head towards the Hero, her eyes filled with concern, but also a veil of expectancy for what he promised her. On a seat beside the bed, resting on a handkerchief, was a pile of dried, elongated leaves, illuminated by the light of a single candle.

Hansio was deaf to her implorations, his eyes mesmerized by the sight of her enormous drooping breasts. Ignoring the girl's suffering, he penetrated her brutally from behind, grabbing one of her breasts in his hands.

Suddenly, he withdrew from her, lifted her up and dropped her on the bed. After removing their clothes, he kissed her passionately and leaned over her, immobilizing her with his weight. The girl had trouble breathing and went quiet, her laments silenced for now. Hansio enjoyed the sound of her panting breath and the feel of her large breasts against his chest. After one last kiss, he lifted his head and bit hard into her lower lip, making her bleed. The girl's body writhed in shock and pain. The sudden violent movement created a pleasurable friction.

"I'm bleeding," the girl said, her voice quiet and strangled. A single tear fell from one eye and she trembled, trying not to scream.

Hansio calmed his passion for an instant and focused on the woman's unattractive face. He was still inside her. A trickle of blood colored her lips and dripped into the corner of her mouth, gathering in the fold. The red color shocked him. He felt his own wet lips and licked them. The salty taste lingered on the tip of his tongue, arousing an unknown sensation. The only thing going through his mind was that he wanted more. He bit the girl's lip again. Fighting against him vainly, she scratched him on the chest, but the burning sensation did nothing more than enhance his pleasure. Hansio sought her wounded mouth with his tongue and felt two small cuts. Sucking a little of her blood, he began once again to pound her with his hips. He liked it, it was good— an invigorating nourishment. The energy flowed down his body and between his legs. The thrusts he delivered shook the girl's arched body, and again, he could not keep away from her swollen breasts. He bit into one and avidly sucked the blood. The consistency of the flesh between his teeth suddenly made him remember that day and his excitement diminished. This had never happened to him before. No other sexual act had ever aroused emotions like this. Maybe it was the taste of the blood and the odor of death in the village...

He grunted with anger and tried to distance his thoughts. It gave the girl the reprieve she waited for. Now able to breathe normally, she seized on the opportunity to take advantage of his dismay and tried to slip out from beneath him. Hansio snapped out of his daze just in time to seize her by the hips. The idea that his prey was getting away rekindled his ardor and with the same fury as before he reached a climax without withdrawing from her.

"Babies are born dead near the Frontier," she said bluntly, a reminder more to herself than to the Hero.

* * * *

When he finished, his breathing slightly hurried, he noticed the expression of disgust and pain on the girl's face, accentuated by the trembling flame of the candle.

The woman got out of bed, unchallenged this time, and gathered her clothes. She took two of the dry leaves from the handkerchief and ran towards the door without looking back. All of sudden she stopped and gingerly retraced her steps. She was about to take another leaf when Hansio grabbed her wrist. The Hero felt the girl's body shake with fear. He observed her bleeding breast and still tasted her blood in his mouth. He let go of her trembling arm.

"To not feel the pain," she whispered, as she took another leaf.

"To not feel the pain," echoed Hansio.

When he was finally alone, he took a leaf and got his pipe from his sack at the end of the bed. He crumbled it into the tobacco. "To not feel anything at all," he said to himself, and lit it with the candle.

* * * *

The drug sent him to sleep, but he had not forgotten to keep the Hastur sword by the bed. It was still in its sheath and wrapped in a sheet to stop indiscreet eyes noticing the blue glow.

A thud awoke the Hero with a start. Despite the powerful effects of the drug he still had the light sleep of a warrior. His hand rushed for the hilt of the sword. He remained in bed, his back against the wall. The door was slightly ajar, but a rapid look around the small room calmed him. It was empty and his things all seemed to be in their places.

Then suddenly he heard a voice.

"Hansio of the Gray Sea, Hero of the Dying Lands."

The voice came from a dark corner of the room and Hansio's eyes struggled to focus in the gloom. A man stepped out from the darkness. He was wrapped in a dark cape, his hood flat upon his shoulders.

A blue light shone from his body, a light Hansio had seen in

Alberto Büchi

the past, created by the more powerful of the Hastur, those who claimed they heard the arcane voices of the gods. Hansio was unsure whether what stood before him was a vision or a living entity. The Hasturs' magic could often confuse the mind, even the minds of the Heroes. It was a long time since he had found himself before one of their kind.

"I have come to call you back to your duties as a Hero." The voice was clear, soothing but decisive. Hansio had never heard the voice of a Hastur coming from the mouth of a common man before. This was also how they managed to bewitch the unfortunate.

"I knew you would come," he mumbled.

"Yes. Martos from the Southern Lands is now with the gods. You are the only one left. You are the last Hero."

"Martos was the last Hero. I am not your servant."

"No Hero is a servant of the Hastur. They are servants to humankind." The tone was placid but penetrating.

"Leave, before I run you through with my sword!"

"You swore an oath on your soul and I am here to ask you to respect it," he said, pointing to the blue light near Hansio. "The sword you hold is the symbol of the oath you made. Now we need your help."

"My oath..." Hansio faltered, speaking slowly and deliberately. "I broke that a long time ago. I do not believe in your fairy tales. Men do not have souls. There is nothing beyond this life." He paused. "Nothing is the true sense to life and nothing is what I wish to become."

Although Hansio felt alert and primed, ready to face a thousand living dead, his yellow eyes were listless. He still felt the effects of the drug.

"The Resistance, whatever use it may be, is well represented by the men I saw in this town. You have no need of me."

"It is not to slow down the infestation of the dead that we ask

32

you to honor your oath."

Hansio's brow rose in suspicion. This was unexpected.

"So, what do you want from me?"

"Martos died during a mission on our behalf, an important mission for the Ark."

"The Ark..." Hansio laughed bitterly. "Spare me your drivel about the Great Exodus."

The Hastur ignored the Hero's provocation, adopting an air of moral superiority.

"Martos died, pierced by a stray arrow, while trying to save a child."

"A child?" Hansio's senses sharpened.

"An important creature for the Ark. She has been kidnapped by the flesh merchants. They thought she was an ordinary girl."

"How can a miserable child be important for the Ark?"

"I can tell you only what you will understand. It is a sign from the gods. Your heresy and insanity is so great that we do not require you to accept certain things... What we need is your Hero courage and warrior strength."

Hansio remained silent.

The Hastur took a few steps towards the Hero, his arm outstretched, palm facing upwards. An image of a violent, stormy sea appeared between his slightly curved fingers. The waves were so high they could have split a forty-foot boat in two. The waters were a deep gray. Beyond the rocks, a tower rose in the distance.

"The Gray Sea," whispered Hansio, in sudden recognition. He went to touch the vision but immediately pulled back his hand, as if afraid it would burn his flesh.

"She was kidnapped near your lands, Hansio."

The Hero hesitated a moment, deep in thought. Then he recovered himself, and yelled, "I no longer possess any lands. There is no one left to defend. Get away from me, sorcerer."

The image disappeared and the Hastur withdrew his hand, remaining where he stood. His expression became more resolute.

"Only death or the Hastur can release you from your oath." Hansio had already heard those words. Martos pronounced them. In that instant they took on a different, more unsettling tone.

"That sounds like a threat."

"It is not a threat, it is a pact. Embark on this mission for us, for humanity. Bring us the child alive and when you return your sword to us, we will release you from your oath."

The Hero could not believe his ears. If this was true, he could be truly free. He would no longer hear the voice of his conscience torturing him.

Gripped by a confused rage he snarled, "You're lying!"

The voice was calm. "The Hastur never lie."

* * * *

Hansio looked at his sword in its scabbard and then again at the Hastur surrounded by the blue aura.

"No one has ever gone so far into the Infested Lands, ever. Not even a Hero, and it is there that I must seek her...you are sending me to my death."

"No one has ever gone that far, this is true, but life is too great a gift from the gods to send someone to their death. We are asking you because we believe you are the only one who can succeed. Your recent life as a wanderer beyond the Frontier is proof of this."

Hansio contemplated the Hastur's blue light.

"I'll bring you the child and you will free me from your yoke."

The Hastur reached out a hand again and the image of a girl appeared. Her face had unusual features. Hansio had never seen lineaments of this kind before. She was beautiful. Her eyes were larger than normal, slightly slanted, the iris a deep blue. With her blonde hair and slender frame, she was the expression of sweetness and innocence.

"This is the child you must save. There is little time. Touch the image and leave immediately."

Hansio touched the image with the tip of his finger and understood that the Hasturs' magic had almost certainly ensured the girl's face would be impressed in his memory...for eternity.

Chapter Four

The Hero travelled for three days, sometimes at a steady trot, sometimes galloping.

The pact with the Hastur was made not far from the territory where the girl was kidnapped.

During his voyage, the strange eyes of the child were like a beacon, continually alight in his mind. So intense was the image Hansio wondered whether the sorcerer had manipulated his mind in some unfathomable way.

He headed west, following, where possible, a straight imaginary line towards the Gray Sea. He crossed the Frontier various times on his journey, stopping only as long as it was necessary to eat and rest his stallion. He often slept in the saddle, but only by day. The Hastur had given him some crackers with extraordinary properties. They were tasteless, but just a few bites were enough to satisfy the deepest hunger. Hansio was familiar with this kind of food and he hated it, not only for its provenance but also because it nourished the body in an illusionary manner. It was certainly nutritious, but if he had to eat those crackers for days on end, he would have collapsed to the ground sucked of energy.

At dawn on the fourth day, he finally arrived at the valley that bordered the lands which were once so familiar to him. Hansio looked at the pale sun and then turned his gaze to the west.

He was on the side of a hill and in the distance was a winding river which once gave life to the valley. A frown of disgust crossed his face when he noticed the waters had turned dark. They reminded him he was in the Infested Lands and suddenly even the air became difficult to breathe.

He dismounted the horse and caressed its nose. His body steamed in reaction to the cold and Hansio wanted to thank him for the enormous effort he made. He leaned his brow on the horse's head and whispered a few comforting words to him. During those days, the stallion had torn through the earth with its hooves whenever he had asked. The animal's curvet was far superior to that of any other horse. He did not fear the Infested Lands like the other beasts, even if he could sense the great danger, and he was used to the odor of death that saturated the air. The horse of a Hero was powerful and intelligent.

Hansio broke off a piece of the Hastur cracker, ate a little, and then gave some to the stallion.

The Gray Sea was nearby, but not yet close enough to see. Even so Hansio almost felt the salty air seep into his nostrils and lungs. He closed his eyes and stood before its tempestuous waves.

The glow of his sword brought him immediately back to the oppressive air of the hillside, before certain memories could overwhelm him.

"We have to move on. We have no time to confront the living dead now," he told the horse, which seemed restless, as if it had also noticed the sword's alarm.

As he rode along an old track that descended from the hill, he glimpsed something that left him speechless. Initially he thought his eyes were deceiving him. By the shores of the river a small group of men followed the water course, heading straight into the bowels of the Infested Lands. A small horse or mule pulled a cart alongside them. They could not be lost, because the river allowed them to orientate themselves perfectly. They walked almost fearlessly, as if they were not more than a league from the Frontier. Hansio decided to follow them.

* * * *

Two days from here, following the river north-east, lay a village. For a while, it had been a stronghold of the Resistance, but had eventually been abandoned. The first to

37

leave were the inhabitants, followed later by many of the warriors. It always happened in the same way. The living dead appeared in great numbers and the incursions of the Hooded Ones were far too frequent. The end of that village was the beginning of many other tragedies for those lands. Willing or not, Hansio remembered it well, because his castle stood nearby. Maybe they were heading there...

Hansio arrived at the river and made his way, leading his horse on foot.

The sparse bushes were whitened by the brine, creating a disturbingly spectral scene.

He kept his distance from the group so they would not notice him.

Suddenly, they stopped. Hansio checked his sword and realized it was glowing blue, but it was not yet intense enough to fear an immediate attack of hungry flesh eaters.

He left his horse by the shores of the river, in a place where the watercourse seemed to vanish into the ground.

The animal stretched its neck towards the water but recoiled immediately with a huff.

"Calm down...it's all right," Hansio urged, in a low voice.

After calming the horse, he cautiously approached the group and found a place where he could spy on what was happening without being seen. What he saw confirmed his fears. They were flesh merchants. The cart pulled a wooden cage with four or five people inside. The torn clothes looked as if they belonged to women and the prisoners he managed to see had long hair. In front of the cart were four armed men, wearing large bands of fabric in front of their noses, no doubt soaked in perfumed essences to allow them to bear the foul stench of the Infested Lands. They stood immobile as if waiting for someone.

Soon someone arrived.

Hansio could not see very clearly, but the men immediately

seemed nervous. They took a step back and one of them jumped onto the cart.

The Hero clenched his teeth until they ground together. His attention turned to the luminous glow of the sword, which was growing more intense.

Lying flat on the ground, he watched closely as a hooded figure appeared before the group, surrounded by a dozen or so living dead who were under his command.

Hansio studied the situation. He had no intention of intervening. His mission was not to stop flesh trafficking.

Looking at the wagon again, he saw a figure smaller than the others, huddled against the posts.

That figure could be a child.

This changed everything.

The Hero reflected a moment on ten living dead, a Hooded One and four men who would definitely retaliate if he intervened. The men did not look like warriors.

One of the merchants walked towards the Hooded One and after a few words, retreated, backing away. Clearly he did not trust turning his back on those beings.

Hansio had no reason to wait any further. Pulling out his dagger and letting out a whistle, he burst into the open, spinning the weapon one hundred and eighty degrees in the air and gripping the blade. Their eyes turned upon him in an instant. The merchant on the wagon froze and the Hero, who was just a few steps away, hurled the knife at him. The short blade sank into his chest with a dull thud. The others hesitated a second, disorientated by the sudden apparition of the Hero, and reacted only when they saw their companion fall from the wagon.

Hansio blocked the first clumsy attack and retaliated, hacking the hip of one of the merchants, breaking his spinal column. A stream of hot blood spurted out, thawing the frost on a dry bush. Hansio turned his gaze to the group of living dead and saw a number of them coming towards him, excited by the blood.

The last two flesh merchants attacked him at the same time. He blocked the violent assault of the first and anticipated the blow of the second by kicking him in the stomach. However, he was immediately forced to deflect a direct hit to the head, and taking advantage of the missed blow and the imbalance of the aggressor, he dealt a punch with his free hand. He heard the sound of broken bones and the face of the merchant became a contorted mask as his jaw broke. A couple of teeth fell to the ground, mingled with saliva and blood. The man dropped his sword and brought his hands to his face, groaning with pain. He could not close his mouth, even when he tried to push his chin up with both hands. In chorus with the merchants' guttural cries, Hansio heard the growls of the living dead, who were famished and increasingly more excited by the scent of blood. They were already closing in.

There was one man left, the one he had kicked away, but he had already fled in terror. Hansio despised cowards, but he could not blame him. It was obvious he was no warrior and his companion with the broken jaw already had the living dead upon him. They had forced him to the ground and three of them were already bent over with his fresh flesh between their teeth. That sight would have terrorized anyone.

Hansio jumped towards the wagon where the body of the merchant he had pierced with his dagger now lay. He extracted the blade from his chest and threw it with all his might at the fugitive. The blade hit him straight between the shoulder blades.

The smell of the living dead was growing stronger and as he turned he was forced to jump backwards before two gnarled hands seized him by the throat. Hansio stepped to one side, lashed out with his sword and cut off the limbs of the creature. The blow stopped the being in its tracks, giving the Hero time to attack.

He danced with his sword, moving with quick feet and coordinated arm movements. In one swoop he chopped off the head of the handless corpse and drove his blade above the ear of the one closest to him.

All that remained were three, who were intent on tearing the merchant's body to pieces, and the other five who had remained near the Hooded One.

Hansio had time to decide whether to attack the first three or the one who was commanding them with his mind. The Hooded One had already turned his back and was leaving in an apparently calm manner. The other five corpses were released from the invisible chains that shackled them, following the scent of flesh and blood.

Hansio checked the prisoners in the cage, who were terrified but unharmed.

He tensed his hands around his sword and advanced quickly towards the three that were feeding. Two were decapitated with extreme ease, while the third came much too close. Hansio moved to one side, tripping on the remains of the merchant. He had enough of his wits about him to keep his sword in his hand, holding it in front of him as he fell. When the being hurled itself at him, the point of the blade went straight through one of its black eyes. Hansio freed himself of the fetid corpse that fell on him and prepared to fight the remaining five.

The Hooded One had already vanished from sight. They could return to their cove for now. Hansio was interested only in the prisoners; or rather, the littlest one.

Hansio was charged, flushed and angry. He took a deep breath and exhaled. The sword was covered in blood and released an intense blue light. A foul red liquid dripped from the tip of the blade onto the ground. His hands were firmly clenched around the hilt and as the anger rose within him he unleashed his wrath again.

He scalped the first, decapitated the second, and then stepped backwards. The last three were close to each other. He should be able to eliminate one of them without the others grabbing hold of him. This was possible only if he kept in constant motion. Wielding his weapon in both hands, he struck again and tore off the head of the one to the right, then took a quick step in the same direction. He raised his sword and gave a diagonal blow to the skull of the last but one. As the body slumped over, the top half of its head slid slowly to the ground.

Only one now remained. It managed to grab his left arm. Its teeth tried to snap at him, but Hansio struck its face with the hilt of his sword. He had to hit out a second time to make the creature fall back, then he slashed out with his sword and half an arm dropped to the ground. The living dead was unstoppable and felt no pain, forcing Hansio to make a swift, deft movement, definitively splitting its rotten head in two. Finally, the Hero stopped.

The massacre was over.

If the Hooded One had remained to control them it would have been far more difficult, he thought, his gaze roaming into the distance.

* * * *

The women in the cage stared at him in astonishment and terror. The light of the Hastur sword had almost extinguished. He freed the prisoners, who crawled from the cage on weak, stiff legs. The Hero's yellow eyes seemed so devoid of humanity that they were too afraid to speak.

Hansio pushed two of them aside and ventured into the cage. Curled up in a corner, shrunken with cold, was a small girl. He grabbed her chin and scanned her face. It was not the Hasturs' child.

Never mind, Hansio thought. If the flesh merchants had organized an exchange here, it was likely the Hooded One wanted to take the 'meat' to the village in the north-east.

* * * *

Hansio gathered all the bodies and limbs of the living dead and put them in a pile. He removed the clothes from one of the bodies and made a sack from the shreds of fabric. One of the creatures had a gash in its side from the day it had died and Hansio tore out some of the entrails and put them in the improvised sack. The smell made his stomach turn.

Even though it looked unlikely they had been bitten, he chopped off the heads of the three flesh merchants near the wagon and put their remains with the others.

He also went to recover the body of the escapee he had knifed between the shoulder blades. He put his foot on his back and pulled out the knife. A rattling wheeze came from the body. Hansio was surprised that he was still alive and turned him over. He looked as if he could still speak.

"Why do you do this?" Hansio asked.

"To...help me..."

"Why do you do it?" he repeated, showing no pity.

Suffering did not move him, pity did not touch him. All he wanted was an answer to his question.

"They...they breed..." The weak voice was now becoming a gurgle.

"I know this. Why have you lowered yourself to making pacts with them?"

"Our...village. They don't attack the village..."

The yellow eyes became more acute. "Of course...you can deal with a few living dead but fifty, a hundred of them, maybe controlled by the Hooded Ones...no, definitely not."

Hansio took his dagger and slit his throat.

Hansio understood, and as the man died at his feet he came to the conclusion that they did the most logical thing they could. Moral condemnation was not his place. Besides, he might do the same in their position.

He cut off his head and cast it onto the pile.

The sight of the sun placated his fury. There was not much time. He could not light a fire. His purification ritual could not be done.

A child would not be used for breeding, at least not straight away, at least not before the first blood, but as food...

Hansio returned to retrieve his horse, tied the sack with the corpse entrails to the saddle and mounted. He had to reach the village in the north-east as soon as possible.

As he passed the wagon he noticed the group of prisoners staring at him expectantly. They watched him the whole time, apparently unable to fend for themselves.

"Where are you going? Why are you going north?" a sobbing woman cried.

Hansio did not understand the question. "What do you want from me?"

"You saved us...your eyes and your sword reveal you are a Hero..."

"I am not a Hero. Go back to your homes."

"How? We are women and we do not know how to travel in the Infested Lands."

Hansio reflected a moment. "That is no concern of mine."

"We will face certain death. They will attack us and transform us..."

"Gather the weapons you see on the ground and use the merchants' mule to help you. There is nothing more I can do for you."

He spurred his horse and left.

Chapter Five

Hansio had to tilt the water sack almost vertically to release
the last drop. He pulled back his head and opened his mouth.
He looked at the leaden sky and his eyes met the sun. The
last precious drop finally moistened his tongue.
It was getting colder.
The sun was still there in the sky, pale and tired, the same as
the day before. Maybe it would snow soon.
I wonder what will happen when it dies too, he thought. The
inevitability brought with it a refreshing sense of calm.
Hansio squeezed the sack and got another unexpected and
fortuitous drop. A seagull appeared, swooping across his line
of vision. The Hero was close to the rocks where they made
their nests. With his head still back, he closed his eyes and,
even though he knew it would be in vain, lifted the water
sack to his lips one more time.
He straightened his head and looked into the distance,
towards the Gray Sea.
Maybe the water had not been contaminated out to sea. If so,
the birds on the rocks would always be able to find food...far
from the land. This hopeful thought irritated him.
He shifted his gaze and could just make out the first houses
of the village towards the horizon. Beyond the rooftops to the
south was the top of a castle tower. That building had
haunted him for a long time and he immediately looked
away.
These lands had once been his. The castle once belonged to
him.
The surrounding area was a succession of small hills and
ridges covered in dry shrubs. His palace was built in ancient
times on one of them.
From a distance, the village seemed deserted yet the Hastur
sword was already glowing.

Hansio dismounted the stallion.

There must be hundreds of them, he thought.

He placed his hand on the hilt. He could feel its vibrations under his palm. The sword was crying out, hungry for the blood of the living dead.

It was still daytime and the Hooded Ones did not like the light. Hansio had no idea why, and even the Hastur seemed to know little about them. Maybe they simply preferred to come out at night. All anyone knew was that they wore capes, stolen from transformed and devoured corpses.

A long time ago, when he was part of the Resistance in a camp to the north, not far from where he now stood, Hansio had a close encounter with one of them. It wore a sackcloth, typical of the lower ranking Hastur, the ones that lived in close contact with the people, who were dedicated to helping the community rather than 'talking with the gods'.

Hansio remembered its milky, iris-less eyes, and its hands with three clawed fingers. He tried to run it down but was forced to fend off an attack of the living dead, who had come to defend it.

One of the only other things known about the strange beings was their ability to control the living dead, using a mysterious form of magic or mental ability.

Legend told of a long-gone era in which the Hooded Ones did not exist and the dead remained beneath the ground. One day, the first beings appeared as if from nowhere and the contamination began. It spread inexhaustibly, like a sickness without a cure, more terrible than any plague. Some stories claimed the Hooded Ones had once been human.

There were many tales of the past and the only common elements were the Hastur, preoccupied with the Great Exodus, and the sun that had begun to die.

It was hard for Hansio to imagine that more innocent time, before the lands were pillaged and poisoned beyond all recognition.

He caressed the stallion's face as they followed a footpath
that had almost been eroded by time. It led to a place where
he hoped to leave his horse while he went to the village. He
found the cave he remembered behind a hillock. It was small,
and slender plant roots draped down from above.

Fortunately, it was empty. He tied his horse and took only
his sword, dagger and the sack containing the entrails of the
living dead. Despite the cold, he left his gray fur behind. It
would have impeded his movements and made it difficult to
hide. He needed to feel agile and invisible.

He also needed to feel strong, and so he chewed on a piece of
cracker.

A Hastur in this position would have used the time to recite a
prayer to the gods. Instead, Hansio studied his horse and its
faint signs of nervousness. Hansio had left him many times
before, but this time, the stallion was at far greater risk and
the horse seemed to know it.

The thought that he could be abandoning his precious steed
to its death brought pain to the Hero, but he had no choice.
Hansio stopped caressing him and left.

Once outside, to avoid disturbing the horse any further, he
opened his sack with its gruesome contents. He took the
brunt of the first wave of stench, hoping it would pass
quickly. Then he put his hand inside the sack and covered
himself with the decomposing matter, to mask the scent of
his living flesh as much as possible.

He was surprised how quickly he managed to get used to the
repulsive odor. Then, he surveyed the landscape ahead of
him.

Hansio saw the castle perched near the rocks on top of a
ridge between two rises of land. When he abandoned that
place it was surrounded by the dead. A few bodies had
already started to reawaken, the wind carrying the odor of a

new and imminent wave of Hooded Ones and living dead. Hansio leaned his shoulder against the wall of a house. It was odd that he had not seen any signs of movement. The Frontier was much more 'lively' by comparison.

He wandered silently around the outskirts of the village. The houses were like empty shells of damp stone. There were many abodes and workshops, but they no longer seemed reminiscent of human life.

He continued to explore the perimeter, until he finally saw something move between two houses. To his surprise, it was a little girl. She clutched a rag doll, its one remaining leg dragging along the ground.

Watching the child from behind, Hansio decided to follow. She seemed lost, but her walk was normal and she did not sway or stagger uncertainly like the living dead. He cautiously moved closer, but all of a sudden she disappeared out of sight around a corner.

He shuffled along the wall and poked his head out to look. The little girl was on her knees, crying.

Hansio's heart pounded. He was amazed just to see a child still alive.

"Little one! Turn around, don't be afraid..."

Hansio reached out a hand.

"Don't cry. I'm here now. I'll save you," he said, troubled by the girl's sobs.

"If you make a noise they'll hear us," he whispered.

He touched her shoulder. The girl turned around. Her face was normal, apart from a few wrinkles and her eyes, which bled both blood and tears. The child moaned suddenly and opened her mouth. Hansio swiftly pulled his hand away. He had been tricked by such a cry before. She was hungry.

Hansio backed away incredulous, almost afraid. The child walked towards him and the Hero of the Dying Lands found it hard to accept that it was a little girl. Finally, he came to his senses and remembered what he needed to do. The child was already dead. He drew his dagger from its sheath and drove it into her tiny forehead. Suddenly the child's appearance changed. She became the image of the child he was searching for and it prompted in the Hero a deep sense of urgency.

Shocked, Hansio gripped the handle of the dagger angrily. He extracted the blade and the creature finally fell, and collapsed over its rag doll.

Filled with rage, he stood there contemplating the body, forcing himself to stay calm. For the first time he found no pleasure in killing one of those beings.

She was clutching a doll, he told himself. She was suffering from hunger—she was dead.

Hansio could not afford to stand there and think and he pushed the darkest of the thoughts from his mind.

She was not the first child whose head he had been forced to smash in, but he could not find peace.

He picked up the tiny body and dragged it behind the house into a field that had probably once been an allotment. Grabbing an arm and leg he swung the dead child in the air, throwing her as far away as he possibly could. When he returned he found the child's doll lying on the ground, limp without its owner. Something within the Hero made him pick it up and place it under his belt. A meaningless gesture. He pushed the episode with the little girl to the back of his mind. The village looked otherwise deserted and the Hero could not fathom why. A surreal silence reigned. A sign of a faded horseshoe still hung above a blacksmith's workshop. Many of the surrounding buildings were without windows or doors, like dark, dank caves. It was certainly not what he had expected. Every now and then the Hastur sword let out an intense blue light. He had rarely seen it so bright and this could mean only one thing.

His muscles were tense, ready to spring into action.

Moving cautiously, Hansio looked through the low windows of the houses. From the outskirts he ventured further into the village.

The first buildings looked empty, as if uninhabited for some time. Then he found something unusual. One house at first appeared the same as the others, but when he looked through the window he noticed four beds lined up. What most surprised Hansio was they were in the kitchen.

At the back of the house was a small barnyard. The Hero jumped over the wall to investigate. As he landed, something gave under his feet and he heard the unmistakable crack of breaking bones. Crouching against the wall to hide, he suddenly realized the yard was scattered with bones and mud. Some were white and others seemed older. Mixed in with the mud were human remains.

Trying not to make a sound, he made his way to the kitchen door.

The smell of blood was even stronger inside.

Hansio examined the beds, lifting the covers with the point of his sword. They were soaked with fresh and partly dried blood. He looked around him, perplexed. He walked into the neighboring room, and found another five beds. On two of them, two women lay on their backs. They were naked, their legs wide open. A large gash went from between their legs up to their navels. Hansio moved closer, struggling to maintain his composure. He noticed the nipples of their large breasts were circled with dark aureoles, like those of pregnant women. The flesh of their stomachs looked as if they had been torn open with nails, not with a knife. It had not been long since their gruesome deaths. The bodies were still warm to the touch.

He turned away, not wanting to be disturbed by the scene any longer. There was nothing more of interest to find here.

As he slipped through the same door he entered, a sudden noise from a nearby dwelling put him on alert. It was followed by the wooden sound of a door slamming shut. Hansio guessed it came from a door that led onto the street. He shuffled his back along the wall until he got a decent view of the road.

A Hooded One dragged the lifeless body of a woman by the hair. She appeared to have met a similar fate to the women inside the house. As the creature walked, a trail of blood and pieces of entrails scattered across the ground. Suddenly, it all became obvious to Hansio. The houses in that part of the village were being used for the victims who had been impregnated by the Hooded Ones.

Hansio kept his gaze on the being until it entered another, much larger building which looked like an artisan's workshop.

There were still no signs of life anywhere else in the village. He still remained cautious as he approached the building and peered inside. The Hooded One and the dead woman were nowhere to be seen, but the atmosphere had changed. A sense of discomfort gnawed invisibly at his instincts.

Abandoning caution, he decided to enter.

The door creaked, but after a moment of hesitation Hansio slipped through the small opening.

The air was different. He felt tangible difference on his skin like an irritating vibration.

There was no furniture and patches of damp and moss marred the remaining plaster and stone of the bare walls. He recognized a dark streak on the floor that went in and out of another room, to a door that led to the back of the house.

As he stepped forward, the disturbing vibration grew stronger, as if there was an agitated swarm of insects nearby. Undeterred, he followed the dark trail. Suddenly, what had been a vibration became something more audible.

He stood petrified in the doorway to the second room, his heart pounding hard in his chest as it did at the start of an unexpected battle. He was on guard, ready to fight. He turned around, wielding his weapon in front of him.

He was surrounded by living dead. The second room was crammed with them.

They were lined up against the wall. Some of them had horrific amputations or wounds. As if teetering on the edge of a precipice, Hansio stiffened and did not move a muscle. There were too many of them and the space was too small. His breathing grew faster and shorter, but the arm that carried the weight of his drawn sword was steadfast.

After the initial moment of shock, Hansio did not want to believe his eyes. He resorted to reason, and even though his breathing was still short, he swiftly recovered his composure. They all faced the wall, immobile, a subdued, snarling murmur coming from their throats. The air vibrated with the same intensity.

The feeling of alarm was replaced by a morbid curiosity which, despite his instincts, made him step closer. His change in position had no effect. The only evident reaction was a slight increase in the intensity of the guttural sound they produced. Their eyes were wide open and fixed on the wall. Hansio was safe—for now. As long as they stayed that way they would not pose a threat.

His heart still racing, Hansio left them to their indefinable slumber and continued to follow the trail of blood. Outside, the tracks disappeared into a well-like opening in the ground, covered with a few planks of wood. One of the planks had been moved. Underneath, a faint light revealed a flight of stairs. Without a second thought, the Hero descended and found himself in what appeared to be an underground warehouse. The stench was unbearable, but these days he was far more repulsed by the smell of fresh blood than dead flesh. The weak light came from a torch on the wall, but it was insufficient to gauge the exact size of the room. The glow of the Hastur sword came to his aid, allowing him to see a few steps ahead.

The first thing he made out was a number of dark, thin lines on the right. Initially he thought they were hanging ropes, but then realized they were chains with barbed hooks. They looked wet. Hansio reached out, and found them slimy to the touch. He held his sword closer and realized it was blood, not water. He also suddenly became aware of the slow dripping sound they produced, a sound which surrounded him. There were certainly many more he could not see. It was strange he had not heard it until then. Something hung from another chain. It had an irregular shape and Hansio, curious, moved closer. Initially he did not realize the nature of the shapeless mass. He soon recognized the grossly disfigured torso of a man, whose legs, arms and entire pieces of muscle had been removed. Even his cheeks had been stripped of flesh. The body swung slightly. A tangled mass of entrails hung from a gash in the man's stomach.

Hansio's head spun, but he did not let himself be perturbed. This was exactly what he expected to find. He clenched his teeth and ventured further in.

The silhouette of a doorway emerged through the gloom. He held out his weapon. Something moved slowly on the ground. He pointed his sword and saw what resembled a human being. It was extremely thin and dragging itself towards him. It did not look like one of them. It was not. This was simply an exhausted, dying man.

The man tried to touch him but Hansio moved aside, his foot colliding instead with something else. Using his sword as a torch, he made out another person, in the same condition but not as thin. Suddenly, he realized with shock that he was surrounded by live men and women. All were prisoners. One of them managed to touch him feebly on the back of his neck. For a second his mind betrayed him, the darkness and his own tortured memories playing tricks. Believing he was surrounded by living dead he instinctively lashed out with his sword.

It was only when the blade sank in that he realized he had cut the man's throat. Hansio staggered backwards. This was an incredible sight even for him. This village with its horrifying absurdities was slowly eroding his self-control. Hands reached out, others gripped him. Someone let out a moan. The others echoed.

"Be quiet," he whispered nervously, but his presence had already caused a commotion. Gripped by panic, he twirled his sword, chopping off an arm and partially decapitating a woman. He inflicted other wounds, of which he could not see the full extent in the dark. Someone groaned with pain. They did not have the strength to scream. Hansio sliced at the sound.

* * * *

Apart from a few feeble laments, silence fell again.

Meat for slaughter, he thought. That is what these people are. Food reserves for the Hooded Ones and their walking dead.

He moved among the hopeless bodies. They were no longer human. A small shape curled up next to a still body. Instinctively he moved towards it and leaned over.

The light of the Hastur sword illuminated the body of a dead woman. Her eyes were open wide. By her side was a child, who seemed unconcerned by his presence. The girl prodded the dead woman with a finger as if trying to rouse her from a deep sleep. With a flash of strange intuition, Hansio grabbed the child roughly to get a better look.

Two large eyes of an unusual shape gazed back at him.

This was the child he was looking for.

Hansio could not believe his luck. He hesitated a moment, but it was definitely her. She was naked but appeared to be unharmed, with no obvious wounds.
Her defenselessness touched him, knocking him off-guard.
One look was enough. Something stirred deep inside him.

Chapter Six

Hansio felt both enchanted and amazed. The child looked so frail, yet even her skin, ravaged by the cold of the Infested Lands, was still unmarked, without even a bite or scratch. She had survived until his arrival.

The emotional impact on the Hero was heightened by an undecipherable expression in those large, slanted eyes, which sent him reeling.

She did not utter a word and returned to contemplating the lifeless woman.

A subdued murmur in the background caused Hansio to turn his yellow eyes away from the child.

The noise, a faint muttering, was mostly indecipherable but Hansio just made out two words, "Save us…" He could not tell if the sound came from the man curled up on his right or if it came from someone behind him.

"Save us…" the voice begged again.

Vaguely irritated, Hansio refused to listen.

He had hesitated and allowed himself to get caught up in the horrors of this village and the misery of this butcher's meat for far too long.

He picked the girl up and tried to drag her away. Her body was freezing. Maybe he had arrived just in time.

The girl still did not speak or make a sound, but clung desperately to the woman she thought was asleep. Hansio pulled at her and the tiny hands lost their grip.

In one arm he had the child. With the other hand he held out the Hastur sword in front of him.

As they made their exit, the little girl continued to look behind her, but she did not get upset or cry at the forced separation. Hansio felt her chin on his shoulder and tried to picture the sad expression in those big eyes.

The light of his weapon illuminated the undulating human

quagmire in which he was immersed. The path he created was immediately covered by a mass of slithering, crawling or begging people. Some of the voices became higher than the others. Some of them got on their feet. Hansio had already told them to be quiet. Maybe they preferred the rapid death of his sword over an uncertain escape.

He could not and did not want to listen to them, putting an end to every sign of pity before it could even begin.

He realized he had lost his bearings in the dark underground cavern and the prisoners on the floor showed no desire to move. Hansio advanced with cold determination, pushing and crushing underfoot anyone who got in his way. He took the first direction that instinctively came to mind, but immediately found himself at a dead end, a damp wall of rock, surrounded by groaning people.

He retraced his steps, ignoring the hands that tried to stop him. He kicked out, trampling on a head and numerous limbs. Then all of a sudden the cries ceased.

Hansio froze. The human meat was backing away, pressing themselves against the walls. It looked like the tide on one of the rare beaches of the Gray Sea.

Only one thing could provoke such a reaction. A Hooded One was coming towards them. Hansio threw the glowing sword aside and crouched among the prisoners on the opposite side of the room. He drew the child, who remained strangely calm, close to his chest.

Hansio recognized the sound of the Hooded One's steps and its silhouette suddenly take shape in the dark. The being was not wearing a hood and its head looked smooth and round. The milky white eyes glowed in the darkness, as if lit by a faint luminescence of their own.

The Hero imagined those two white dots could target a precise strike even in these dark conditions.

He could not allow that to happen, not now, not with the

child so close to him.

The Hooded One looked left and right, sniffing the air. Its gaze hovered over the point where Hansio crouched. He moved slightly, trying to hide behind a prisoner who was clawing at the flesh of a neighbor, in a vain attempt to find a safer hiding place.

The monster growled quietly and took a step forward. Hansio braced himself. His hand reached for his dagger and the muscles of his arm flexed. He was about to extract the weapon but stopped. The Hooded One was attracted to a glare in the darkness—the Hastur sword.

The ruse worked. The creature growled again and moved towards the blue glow of the Hastur blade, pushing the prisoners he met on his short journey aside, kicking the slower ones. When the being reached the sword it paused, as if afraid to touch it.

Hansio took advantage of the moment of hesitation. He left the child and hurled himself towards the enemy. Sensing his presence, the Hooded One turned. Its inhuman snarl pained Hansio's ears as he plunged the dagger into its neck. The creature dodged the assault but the Hero picked up his sword and waved it menacingly. The blue light fleetingly illuminated the monster's face and for the first time Hansio got a good look at one of them. The first thing he noticed was its crescent-shaped mouth. It had no lips and its sharp, black teeth were not set in soft skin and gums. Instead, the roots were sunk directly into its jaws. Its strange inhuman smile went from ear to ear.

Clearly irritated by the Hastur light, the Hooded One moved aside, but did not refuse the fight. It used its claws as blades. Each hand had three bulges that looked like five human fingers fused into three digits.

Hansio felt the flesh of his chest tear and a sudden burning sensation. He was hurled back but did not fall. He swung his sword clumsily in the air to stop the creature from pouncing on him, wielding it in front of him.

The Hastur blade illuminated the top of the Hooded One's head, covered in straggly white hairs as long as a palm, and the skin of its skull seemed to be calcified.

Hansio lashed out with his sword but missed the target and the creature nimbly disappeared.

The Hero found himself plunged into darkness and even the prisoners had stopped moaning.

A slight current of air was all that preceded the Hooded One's surprise attack from the rear. He twisted his body and the hilt of the sword crashed against the creature's teeth.

Stunned by the blow, the monster was thrown backwards. Without hesitation, Hansio pierced through its body in an upwards motion.

The blade entered just below the breastbone and thrust out behind its shoulder blade.

The Hero's fury was so great that the Hooded One remained suspended in the air, skewered on his sword.

The blue light now fully illuminated the horrendous features of the being and the fleeting glimpses that Hansio had before were revealed in all their horrifying glory.

Noticing fresh blood on its chin, he asked, "Have you just eaten?"

Still alive, the Hooded One let out a strangled cry that the Hero interpreted as a malevolent laugh.

"That belongs to the woman you were dragging, doesn't it? Her flesh was tender..."

The Hooded One vomited a dark liquid, its own putrid blood.

"I too tasted the flesh of a woman a long time ago."

With those last words the muscles of Hansio's arms relaxed. He freed his sword, hurling the being against the wall of rock. It landed with an unexpectedly muffled thud as its deformed body hit some of the prisoners.

The cuts on Hansio's chest burned furiously, but his first thought was his mission. Hansio turned towards the child and found her standing gazing vacantly ahead. He searched for the Hooded One, intending to finish their battle by decapitating it, but the creature had vanished. He took the child in his arm and scanned the darkness for an exit. It was not long before he found the stairs out of the subterranean slaughterhouse.

Hansio came back into the open with a sense of relief. He looked for the sun, trying to ascertain how long he had been below ground. It was nowhere to be seen in the gloom, but the leaden gray of the sky suggested snow would soon fall. Small white dots, carried by the wind, already drifted through the air. There was still enough light to make his escape, but he had to hurry.

He focused his senses on the hum of the slumbering dead inside the workshop, hoping they remained inactive.

The surreal atmosphere felt unchanged.

He took a step forward and felt an acute pain in his neck, a sudden burning sensation. His breath was too short to cry out and the girl slipped from his arms. He fell to his knees and swiftly twisted his upper body round to find the source of the pain. It was the Hooded One. The creature had caught up with him and a sliver of freshly torn meat dangled from its needle-like teeth.

The Hero's eyes opened wide in disbelief.

That could not be his flesh between its teeth.

He touched his neck and felt something wet. The burning grew worse. Holding up his hand, he saw his own blood.

He turned to the child who gazed back with her usual empty expression, stunned and lost, as if she could not comprehend the implications of the wound.

Hansio's attention returned to the Hooded One and he wrinkled his brow in disgust as he watched it chew and swallow the bleeding flesh.

The anger that fueled him each time he clashed with these beings helped him to react. He raised one knee and then the other and got back on his feet. The creature leapt towards him with outstretched claws, its jaws wide open.

Hansio was brutal.

He exploited the monster's leap to grab it by the throat. Lifting it off the ground, he squeezed its neck so tightly that his fingers sank into its throat. The dark blood that poured from the Hooded One's wounds had a corrosive effect on the skin and Hansio's hand burned. He did not release his grip. He felt the cartilage and bones shatter. The pressure inside its skull was so strong that its white eyes almost popped out of their sockets. The Hooded One tried to break free, scratching at Hansio's face, trying to blind him with its three clawed fingers.

Finally, the neck broke and the body slumped, but Hansio was still not satisfied. He threw the monster forcefully to the ground and smashed its skull with a furious blow from the hilt of his sword.

The Hero was exhausted. The scratches burned his skin like acid and the bite on his neck...he did not want to think about it.

He scooped up the child, and rushed into the workshop.

As soon as he crossed the threshold he realized something had changed, the living dead were awake. The dead Hooded One must have freed them, Hansio thought angrily. Some were scratching the wall as if trying to dig their way out. Others were banging their heads as if the wall did not exist. It was almost as if they were gripped with dismay at the loss of the telepathic intelligence that once controlled them. Meanwhile, others had already turned around, and were looking at the Hero and the child with hungry eyes. Hunger had become their only intelligence.

Hansio twirled his sword and smashed two of their heads. One managed to grab his sword arm. With an abrupt shoulder movement, Hansio freed himself from its grasp. He smothered a cry of pain. The bite from the Hooded One was the most painful thing he had ever felt, but he did not want to leave the child behind and he had no inclination to give in to those monsters.

His sword dislodged another skull and, behind the body that fell to the floor, he saw the exit. He picked up the child, leapt over the body and finally reached the open air.

Initially the street seemed deserted, but then he noticed another Hooded One about a hundred paces away. Immediately behind it, more of the living dead were leaving one of the houses. At the same time, another appeared from a nearby doorway, its pack of dead swaying around it.

Hansio clutched the child to his chest and ran in the only clear direction he could.

As he fled he came across three living dead, wandering masterless along the street. Just like the ones from the Frontier, he thought. They lunged towards him and Hansio fought them off with kicks and a few feeble slashes of his sword. In his haste, he did not manage to decapitate one of them. Those damned Hooded Ones must have sensed something. They had hidden inside their houses with their beasts and human food reserves, he thought furiously, darting his eyes around the scene ahead.

All of a sudden, the village had come to life. Hansio was beginning to question whether it had been a good idea to kill the Hooded One that had bit him. If they could communicate with their minds then, sooner or later, all of them would come out of their lairs to rescue their companions. There was a chance they were only after the meat in the underground storehouse, but it seemed unlikely this would be their only priority once they spotted him.

In reality, killing the Hooded One had proved insignificant. The alarm had been raised as soon as the battle beneath the ground began.

Hansio weakened and felt the need to stop, if only for a moment. He slowed his pace. He was out of breath and his wounds— three parallel gashes across his body—really hurt, even the one on his face.

In this part of the village, the houses were piled on top of each other, as if the deformed walls needed one another to hold themselves up, creating a myriad of nooks and hidden corners.

One of the living dead suddenly stumbled from a doorway, but without a foot, which had been devoured up to the heel bone, it fell over. Hansio watched as it got back up and fell down again after only a few steps. There was no point wasting time watching or breaking its skull. It was no threat. Hansio slipped into a space between two houses and paused to catch his breath.

The girl's face reflected his worried and pained expression, her eyes wide as if she still did not understand.

She was a fragile creature and Hansio moved carefully, measuring his strength so he would not crush her in his arms.

Protecting such a delicate being was a new experience. Being a father, he thought-as if he was defending the dearest thing in his life.

The child was no longer just a living creature. She had transformed into a warm and luminous wave of thought in his mind.

It was extraordinary to think that in this awful place where putrefaction of the flesh reigned, this tiny child had become a font of serenity, peace and other alien feelings. He set the child gently down on the ground and studied her. Despite her physical peculiarities, she was perfect. Her arms were longer than usual and her legs excessively slender, but she seemed like any other child.

Hansio felt that something more lay within her; something different. She was covered in his blood, which had poured out from the horrendous gash in his neck and the cuts on his face and chest, but she was not wounded. He turned her around. Not even her back was marked. There were a few bruises, a graze, but no bites or cuts.

The Hero was brought back to reality by the hungry cries of the living dead, who had now picked up his scent. He turned towards the street and saw a group of cadavers coming towards them. They were bashing into each other, squashed against the walls of the narrow passageway.

Fortunately, the other exit was clear. He brandished his sword and decapitated the nearest one. He chopped off the leg of the second and did the same to the next. The hungry, choleric bodies piled up on top of each other, making it difficult for the others to advance.

His arm was tired and the wound on his neck was making his blows weaker and less efficient. After repeated slashes of his sword, Hansio picked up the girl and fled.

* * * *

Darkness was swallowing up the undulating landscape and the Gray Sea in the distance had merged with the mist. Carried by the wind, the first flakes of snow were like needles on his skin. Before they could reach the black stallion, they multiplied, coming down harder and faster. They were caught in a blizzard.

Hansio cast a melancholic gaze towards the tower of the castle, at the mercy of the snow, lashed by the elements and already covered in white. It had become to him the image of powerlessness in the face of the invincible.

Despite this, Hansio wished he could die there and a feeling of warmth spread through his chest at the thought.

He would be dead soon, he knew. It would not be long until he would have to find a way to kill himself before he transformed. It was still not the right time. The feel of the girl's tiny body made him realize that first he would have to escort her as close to the Dying Lands as possible. At the Frontier he would entrust her to the first guard he could find. Was he really obliged to do so? After all, he would be dead soon, so there would be no obligation to respect the pact...

He avoided asking himself any more questions, so he would not be forced to give an answer that was not coherent with his own vision of reality, with the life he had passed before that mission for the Hastur.

He had no clothes to protect the child from the cold, but the horse's hiding place was now close at hand.

On reaching the animal, it was clear it too was suffering from the frigid temperatures. Tiny ice crystals beaded its mane.

He had to get away from these lands as soon as possible. The blizzard would aid their escape by making it hard for the living dead to follow.

He placed his fur over the child's slender shoulders and lifted her onto the horse's back. He mounted behind her, and was overcome with weakness. The blood loss and immense pain at the base of his neck overwhelmed him in a wave that took his breath away. He feebly took the reins and spurred the horse on into the blizzard.

The snow and the mist provided no reference points, so he decided to trust his sense of orientation to reach the river. Once there, all he had to do was follow the shore to the Dying Lands. Blizzard or no blizzard.

Chapter Seven

The blizzard grew stronger and the stallion proceeded at a slow trot, its hooves sinking into the layer of fresh snow. The wind thrashed at their faces.

The child fidgeted beneath the large fur, her head nestled between her arms and legs.

Exhausted, Hansio slouched over the child, his body feebly following the horse's movements. He had never felt a greater pain that the one caused by the bite of the Hooded One. He had suffered bigger and deeper wounds in his youth— particularly on one occasion, when he fought against a group of lawless marauders who assailed one of the villages in the lands to the south.

This bite burnt like acid on raw flesh. The wound was on fire, while the rest of his body suffered the cold of the Infested Lands more than usual. He had lost a lot of blood, but instinct told him that the cause of his sudden weakness was the toxins in the creature's saliva.

His head flopped from side to side in time with the horse's gait, and his eyelids droop over his yellow eyes. At least the child seemed protected from the cold.

With a huge effort, Hansio raised his chin and forced his eyelids open to see what the child was doing. She was still wrapped up, mouth open, her nose pointing up to the sky. Her tongue moved up and down, seeking the snow. Blown by the strong wind, the snowflakes stung her face, forcing her to huddle up under the warm folds of the fur. Hansio had finished his water a long time ago.

With his hands wearily stretched out to hold the reins, he mustered up enough strength to squeeze his arms around her. The two braids of his hair had become icicles and his beard was now thick with ice and snow.

Hansio straightened his back and studied the horizon with

an afflicted, listless expression. He had no idea where he was and was not even optimistic he was on the right road. Not even weakness could force him to give in.

They had not yet met the river, but visibility was so poor they might have passed near its shores without realizing.

The situation forced him to continue in the hope of finding shelter. The stallion displayed such extraordinary stamina that, when Hansio's eyelids finally gave up the fight and closed, he put his faith in his horse, allowing himself merely to be transported like a useless, dead weight. With his hands gripping the reins, his defenseless body remained upright, thanks only to an inbuilt instinct. He was aided too by the cold, which stiffened his muscles. All of a sudden, however, the stallion stumbled over a hole. There was a slight jerk and Hansio slipped to one side. The impact with the ground was fortunately cushioned by the snow.

Now awake, Hansio's head was immersed in white, the snowflakes misting his vision. Moving heavily with fatigue, he wiped his face. The girl was still in the saddle and without its rider, the faithful stallion came to a halt.

In that precise moment, Hansio realized he would not survive.

If he had not been bitten they might have made it, but before him awaited the agony that would bring him death and, inevitably, transformation. What sense was there in going on?

He pushed himself up with his arms and got on his knees. The blizzard covered his legs in a candid coat of white. In that moment, he wanted to die.

Frostbite, however, would not stop the transformation. There was only one way to avoid it.

He searched for his sword, but could not even draw it from his sheath. It was too heavy and his fingers were too numb. His dagger would be lighter and smaller.

He looked at the stallion and the child and pulled out the weapon.

The gaze of his steed and the girl annoyed him, but in a short while it would no longer matter. He would drive the dagger into his head or through an eye. He certainly did not have the strength to break his own skull alone. Slitting his own throat or driving the dagger into his heart would not suffice.

The weapon trembled in his hands and Hansio struggled to keep his fingers around the hilt. He would have to use his own weight to ensure the blade reached his brain.

The child continued to stare at him wordlessly. Suddenly, his annoyance turned to anger. He raised the tip of the dagger towards the sky and bent over, guiding the knife towards his head.

The enormous eyes of the little girl filled with torment and seemed to judge him. It was enough. Hansio could not bring himself to do it.

He dropped the dagger, which vanished into a cross-shaped hole in the snow. If he had been strong enough he would have shouted and scolded the child for having dared lay her eyes upon him. All that came from his mouth was a dejected, muffled cry of pain. He let his body fall backwards and closed his eyes.

The wound on his neck sent unbearable waves of fiery pain through his body that not even the deep, cold snow could placate.

I have to get up, said a voice inside his head. The voice was his own, but seemed to come from someone else.

I have to get up,the voice repeated.

I have to get up.

Disgusted by the nauseating instinct to survive, Hansio got to his feet.

He plunged his hands into the snow to retrieve his dagger.

Moving with great heaviness, he headed towards the stallion

and had to grip the trappings to stop himself from collapsing. He rested his head on the horse's flank.

Since they escaped the village the wind had not stopped for an instant, but, for a brief moment, as long as the interval between two heartbeats, the flurry of snowflakes died down. A light came on in the Hero's mind.

Straining his eyes, Hansio gazed out in front of him. Just twenty paces ahead, there was a dark object, a sort of hillock with hazy gray contours.

He gestured to the girl to cover herself and led the stallion towards the mound.

Once they drew closer he realized the object was in fact the top of a door.

The light in his mind transformed into hope.

All around him was white and the wind lashed at their skin. He threw himself to his knees, digging with his hands to move as much snow as he could. Finally, he was at the entrance to a place, which, although it represented death, was a welcome refuge.

They must be in the Valley of Tombs, Hansio realized, where the remains of valorous warriors and kings lay. These men lived in such remote times that their names were long forgotten. Only bones could be found inside these mounds now and, in some cases, not even those. The living dead had no interest in bones, least of all the treasures often concealed in the tombs. This was why this place remained uncontaminated.

However, the discovery also implied the bitter acknowledgement that they found themselves much farther away from the Frontier than Hansio had thought or dared to hope.

We'll never reach the Dying Lands, he thought, but at least my body will turn to dust here. He continued to dig until he had created a hole large enough to force the door of the tomb. With an unexpected surge of new-found energy, with the help of his sword, and to the sound of kicking feet, he managed to make a gap in the snow.

He grabbed the stallion's saddle bag and took the child in his arms. He let her through, then followed with difficulty through the narrow passage. It was not wide enough for the horse, so Hansio made a torch. Wrapping a few shreds of fabric around his sword he made a small flame using some oil and flint that had managed to stay dry in his saddlebag. He ventured into the tomb looking for anything that might help him dig a wider passageway.

A metal shield and double-headed ceremonial axe lay inside, and allowed him to widen the opening. He dug angrily with the shield, his efforts thwarted by the incessant snow.

The sudden burst of strength came as a surprise to Hansio. Just moments earlier he had felt completely empty, deciding to continue for as long as his body would allow. Now he could not bear the idea of leaving the horse to die in the cold. Finally, his hard work paid off and he pulled the animal inside.

He lit a fire in a sheltered area, using whatever he could find of use in the tomb. The current created by the broken-down door allowed the air to circulate, clearing out the smoke. He even found a torch hanging on the wall and he wrapped it with more soaked rags and lit it. He checked that the child was in the warmth and made a bed for them both. Once he had seen to the stallion, he took a piece of Hastur cracker from the sack and a bowl to collect fresh snow for water. He gave the food to the girl and the animal, but when he looked at his own piece in his hand, he hesitated. He realized he was not hungry, so he gave his food to the girl and collapsed next to the fire. He was weary and had a high fever. The burst of digging exhausted him, but it had made him forget his wounds and the fate that awaited him.

Death would surely seize him at any moment.

Before he had time to remember the forthcoming transformation, everything became enveloped in an opaque whiteness and a surreal ringing echoed in his ears. Reality ceased to exist.

* * * *

Hansio found pleasure in feeling his skin pull, his muscles weaken at the rip of his flesh. The pain in his side excited him. Someone had stripped him entirely and the cold gave him an added thrill. He did not want to open his eyes. The darkness of his mind was the best place to enjoy that sensation.

A light movement, like a thousand long hairs, brushed against him, caressing his stomach. Then, another fit of pain took his breath away. However, the moan that came from his mouth was one of pleasure. Someone's fingers were penetrating deep into his flesh.

Drops of warm water wet his lips and his eyelids instinctively opened, revealing a hazy reality. The opening he saw through was small and all Hansio could make out were the lines of a face with large, slanted eyes. More drops moistened his lips, but they missed his mouth, sliding instead towards his neck. He closed his eyes.

* * * *

The hands in the raw gash on Hansio's hip seemed to be searching for something. As they stretched, gripped and tore at his flesh, he felt a sense of painful titillation.

Hansio hoped that those same fingers would move inside the wound on his neck. The pain there was immense, but perhaps their work would also increase his pleasure.

As if someone had read his desires, he suddenly felt a scratch from his lower body all the way up to his neck. The nails scratched away the congealed blood and pus that had formed. The torment was precisely the exquisite pain he yearned for. The wholeness of feeling was so strong he wanted it again, even more intensely, an even greater pain. He did not want to open his eyes.

Hair brushed his face and he felt the touch of cold skin on his shoulder. The brush of a cheek. An odor invaded his nostrils. It was familiar, but he could not place it. A mouth opened and the teeth closed together to tear the flesh, so deeply they touched the bone.

* * * *

The Hero felt a warm sensation on his face. He recognized human warmth and the touch of a caress. He opened his mouth, but did not receive any more water. He was hungry, and had an infinite thirst. He fought against his closed eyelids, his eyelashes and skin encrusted with sleep. Finally, a yellow eye found a small slit to see through. His brain could not make sense of the information it was receiving. He could just about recognize the fire in the flicker of the flames.

The face with the large eyes was bright and the sight of her warmed him far more than the fire. The hand that caressed him touched him again on the cheekbone, relaxing one side of his face, the other still contorted with pain.

* * * *

Then, suddenly, teeth clenched the bone again and his shoulder lifted from the ground. The head that was devouring him rose again to take another bite and when the last fiber of his flesh surrendered, his shoulder and the nape of his neck slumped back down to the ground. He felt a weight on his groin and his excitement grew.

There was no need to open his eyes.

Once again, two fingers were inside the wound on his neck and Hansio heard a rip, like the sound of torn hide. His body was freed of a piece of dangling flesh. The sounds of the teeth made him realize that someone was chewing. Blood dripped onto his chest. The scent hit his nostrils again. It was the unmistakable smell of rotten flesh, but for some unknown reason, Hansio associated it with the scent of a woman, the odor of sex.

Thanks to the gentle warm touches that followed, the force that had relaxed his face spread all over his body. Exposed only to a very limited range of sensations, the Hero's mind, which until then had been unable to formulate a single coherent thought, composed a phrase, I'm dying...

Hansio wanted to express it in words but he could not.

The thought of death brought tears to his eyes. Cruelly, he associated the two words with a memory. He never cried, not even when his wife...he pushed the memory away.

The tears melted the sleep in his eyes and he felt them slide, hot, down towards his ears.

He won the battle with his heavy eyelids and through two small openings he recognized the child.

Once again, she became a luminous beam of light and warm thoughts, a font of serenity and peace.

* * * *

That mouth, a source of pleasure and torment, snapped at him again.

It had torn off a nipple, because there was a new wave of pain from his chest. Two icy lips pressed against the edge of the wound and the mouth quenched its thirst with the stream of blood.

He had still not opened his eyes, inebriated by that combination of sexual satisfaction and pain and the strange notion that made him associate the odor of dead flesh with the scent of a woman.

Hansio now felt able to open his eyes. What he saw deeply aroused him.

She was beautiful, naked, almost completely intact, maybe transformed not long before. Her breasts were firm with a soft appearance. The wrinkles on her face were a sign of beauty and her red eyes were a brilliant source of attraction. She was rubbing herself against him, devouring him.

Hansio was having sex with one of them.

Am I now living dead? he wondered, without a sense of disgust.

He repeated the question over and over again as the dead female moved over him like any other normal woman.

* * * *

He felt yet another touch, this time on his chest, and was suddenly overwhelmed by an unknown force. It pervaded him with an energy that was at once alien to his own human nature, yet innately compatible with his very existence, his flesh.

A desert was made fertile.

An emptiness had been filled, a fluid poured into a space that seemed to have been created for this purpose.

Everything was confused.

The dead woman moved sinuously and Hansio realized he could follow her movements.

He touched her breasts and she responded willingly. He made her lean over him, as he wanted to feel that cold body rubbing against his own. Then he took her hand and led it to the gash on his hip, pressing those fingers into his flesh. He wanted more pain.

The woman resumed her meal, precisely where the Hooded One wounded him the first time.

Chapter Eight

Hansio felt the skin of his neck tighten with pain. His eyes were burning so badly they felt as if they had been washed in boiling water. He could not open them. All he could see was darkness. It felt surreal, vague and obscure but he was sure it was real—that he had somehow been awoken.

Fragments of his encounter with the dead woman resurfaced in his mind.

He wrinkled his brow and his eyelids finally opened, breaking away the sleep in his eyes. Reality slowly took shape, but his vision was poor. Everything was blurred, but he knew one thing, he was definitely alone.

He raised a hand to his eyes, but was forced to stop as a stab of pain shot through his body. He could not even tell where the pain came from. He dared not even breathe until the agony died down.

He realized he was neither cold nor hungry.

Rising to his knees with great effort, he tried to deal with other, specific stabs of pain in his legs, abdomen and arms. Hansio looked towards the fire but saw no flames, not even the warm glow from hot coals. He tentatively reached out an arm and realized that the fire must have gone out.

The room was warm, he thought. The fire has not been out long.

He was unable to focus on his surroundings, but his eyes met with a bright glare. Momentarily blinded, he covered his eyes.

With his hands still shielding his face, he got unsteadily to his feet.

The skin of his neck tugged painfully.

Hansio remembered he had been wounded, but had forgotten how serious it was. Liquid trickled down towards his chest and he raised a hand to his shoulder. His fingers sank into a soft, scab-encrusted mass. The flesh gave off a foul odor, but he did not give it any thought. He stood on both feet, unsteady and weak. Although his eyes stung unbearably, they adjusted to the light source and he took a tentative step towards it. He staggered briefly, but managed to recover himself and take a second and third step. Even the muscles of his back sent excruciating waves of pain through his whole body.

One foot hit an object on the floor, while the other made a crunching sound as it hit the ground. He bent down, recognized his saddlebag and picked up the remains of a Hastur cracker. The sack had tipped open and its objects were scattered across the floor. Drawing closer to the bright light, he realized it was a flaming torch. It was the only light source and appeared to be abandoned on what looked like a shelf. The surface was rough and perfectly level to the touch. He found some grooves with his fingertips and, as he moved his fingers across them, realized they felt like engravings. The tomb, he thought. This must be the tomb in the mound. Hansio wondered how long he had been unconscious. His thoughts again returned to the fire, which was out, but not yet cold.

Suddenly, the snort of an animal interrupted his reverie. A black stallion stood by the stone sarcophagus. It took him a moment to realize the air was saturated with the pungent odor of manure, a stench which Hansio had not noticed until now. It clung to the skin like a humid veneer.

He walked around the sarcophagus, holding one edge with his hand to steady himself. He caressed the ancient stone, trying not to lose orientation. Was the stallion real, or was it his imagination? He could not be sure of anything. For an instant, his eyes dimmed as hope faded, lost in a point that the light of the torch could not reach. Were his eyes playing tricks on him? He reached the corner of the sarcophagus and felt something dry underfoot, a small pile of dung.

Hansio slowly reached the stallion, which stood patiently as he approached, breathing quietly in the dim light. He reached up tentatively to touch the roughness of its mane, which hung to the side of its muscular neck. The sudden familiarity filled Hansio with relief.

"It's you," he whispered, pressing his lips on the horse's coat. "It's you..." he repeated, touching the side of its face. He heard the rough sound of his beard rubbing against its coat, and reached for its soft nose.

The pain still made moving difficult and as he shifted his weight, he made contact with another soft object on the ground.

Recognizing the distinctive texture as his own fur cloak, Hansio saw it was abandoned in the shadow of the sarcophagus and something—or someone—was wrapped inside it. Two folded limbs protruded from a still, rounded form.

There was no sound, which must mean the person was either sleeping or dead, he thought.

He rubbed his eyes once more and gradually, his vision returned.

Now he saw the tiny form wrapped inside the fur was a little girl.

Hansio was stunned, as if reeling from a blow. His mind cleared, and everything suddenly re-emerged from the dark mire of his memory. He saved that child on behalf of the Hastur, who had promised to release him from his oath. Martos was dead and he was now the last Hero of the Dying Lands...

Then, with a surge of dread as he remembered his bite wound, he realized he too would soon surely be dead.

Raising his hand to his neck, he told himself the wound was probably infected, that it would most likely kill him.

Something confused him still. I should be dead already, he thought. I should be among the living dead.

He looked once more at the sleeping child, who was not dead.

If he was living dead then he should be hungry and ripping the girl to shreds to feed his appetite.

His instinct was instead to protect the vulnerable creature. He touched her chin, stooping below the weak rays of the torch. It was inexplicable. He was not one of them. Touching his side, he could not find a gash.

* * * *

Hansio left the child to sleep, the filthy rag doll lying beside her. He could not remember giving it to her.

It was vital that he regain full control over his mind and body. All he felt was a great thirst. Even though the light still bothered him, his eyesight improved almost immediately, and the first thing he did was adjust the torch as the flaming rags were subsiding. He then reorganized the objects on the floor and put them back in his saddlebag. He was pleased to find they had not rolled too far away, allowing him to find them without much trouble.

Despite the improvement in his eyesight, the stabbing pain in his muscles still tormented him. Even the simplest movement was torture.

At the foot of the sarcophagus he found a wooden bowl, which he picked up, wincing. He searched around for a water source.

Illuminating the chamber with the torch, the Hero caught sight of a corridor leading away from the tomb and realized it must go outside, although he could barely remember following it. At the end was a shattered door and a mountain of snow that had tumbled through the opening. Beneath the small upper arch of the entrance, a pale ray of sunlight penetrated through a crack.

Hansio knew the tomb was a good hiding place and had no intention of going outside. He was also aware that he was still not strong enough. He gathered some snow in the bowl and returned to the chamber, taking some fragments of wood from the door.

He hung the torch back on the wall, placing it in its holder, which, in ancient times had probably been used to illuminate the tomb during a solemn funeral ceremony.

He used the flint to reignite the embers of the fire. Groggily, he did not think to use the flame of the torch.

The snow melted and he drank. It tasted vile.

Glancing at the cracker on the floor, he thought it would be a good idea to eat. He placed a piece in his mouth and swallowed. The food made him feel nauseous, so he discarded the rest. Each tiny effort exhausted him and after checking that the little girl was still sleeping peacefully, he curled up on his bed, reflecting again on why he was not dead and why he had not transformed. Each thought was crushed by fatigue. Before he knew it, he had fallen asleep.

* * * *

When he woke, he looked at the fire and realized only a short time had passed. He was still thirsty-really thirsty-and his swollen eyes were once again encrusted with sleep. He rubbed them. They burned. The light still irritated him, but it was starting to become more bearable.

The short rest had helped him recover some of his strength. Now he was able to look around the tomb and take in its treasures. A wealth of riches had been buried alongside the body in the sarcophagus, including the double-headed ceremonial axe and shield he used to break down the door. The walls inside the circular room were stacked to the ceiling with the warrior's precious possessions and tools for the afterlife.

Hansio knew they would not be able to stay there forever,

despite its safety. His indomitable nature drove him to keep going.

Summoning up his strength, he took the Hastur sword to the snow-covered doorway, and dug with the same shield he had used earlier. Soon he had once again created an opening. Moving was laborious, but the stabs of pain were less cutting. The snow had fallen thick and deep and with each step, he sank in drifts up to his knees.

It was daylight and the air was unusually clear. Perhaps the blizzard had somehow cleaned the sky. He saw a number of small mounds in the distance, the domes of other tombs. He decided to climb to the top of his own refuge, but his ascent was slowed considerably by his poor health and the thick mantle of snow. When he finally reached the top, the Valley of Tombs appeared before him. Most of the burial chambers were covered in a white blanket, but the valley was exactly how he had remembered. Large, irregular, arcane, proud. It had been swallowed up by the Infested Lands when he was still a young boy.

The weight of his body made the snow crunch beneath his feet. He looked for the pale sun, immersed in the clear sky, and was struck by how different it suddenly seemed.

Could it still be the same sun, he wondered? Something about it seemed changed, but he could not say why.

Hansio shivered. It was bitterly cold.

His last glimpse at the valley comforted him. There were no living dead or Hooded Ones here.

The sword still emitted a faint blue light, but the Hero was unconcerned. The Valley of Tombs was in the heart of the Infested Lands, after all. He was far from the Frontier, and no Hero had ever got so far and come back to tell the tale. He decided that tomorrow or, at the most, the day after, they would continue on their journey. He settled himself next to the warmth of the fire until a sound disturbed his thoughts.

The child had woken. Her head poked out from behind the sarcophagus.

"Come and sit by the fire," he said gently.

The child did not respond, but opened her eyes wide.

"Do you understand me?"

Hansio realized the girl had not uttered a word since they met, not even during their escape.

"Do you understand what I'm saying?"

The child remained still, half-hidden and hesitant, and did not answer.

"Come here!" he said, gesturing with his hands. Then he took a cracker from his sack and passed it to her.

The child moved slowly towards him. She was dirty, naked and extremely thin and clutched the rag doll by its leg.

Hansio was shocked by her fragility. It was a mystery she managed to survive for so long.

"Take it, eat."

The girl grabbed the cracker and sat opposite Hansio, on the other side of the fire. Her wide eyes fixed on the bowl containing the melted snow and she rushed to drink from it.

"You are covered in filth and manure—it's not hygienic. You could have wounds under that dirt."

The child paid no attention to his words and instead focused on the now empty bowl.

"Are you still thirsty? I'll get you some water."

Hansio searched around for an object that could gather even more snow. On the floor he spotted a gold shield, studded with red gemstones, leaning against a wall. It was big enough for the child to have a bath in.

In ancient times the custom was also to leave food in the tomb and it had once probably been full to the brim with fruit. Now, black dust and some small seeds were all that remained inside.

He picked it up, feeling the ache in his neck as he moved, and went to collect as much snow as he could. On his return the child dashed to the shield and took a handful of snow. It was frozen, but she ate it as if it were cream.

Hansio smiled, his eyes apologetic.

He melted some snow in the bowl and placed it near the fire a while to warm it up. He gestured to the girl to come closer.

"I have to wash you. You can't stay like that."

He took her by the arm and wet a piece of cloth in the lukewarm water.

"It's the cleanest rag I could find. A sponge from the Gray Sea would be better, I know. This snow comes from the skies above the Infested Lands. It's rotten, but it's all we have."

Obediently, the child let the Hero wash away the dirt. Hansio tried to be delicate.

"You were very courageous when I was sick. Other children would have cried. You did not even complain about the cold. I can't explain it, but I have a feeling it was you who kept the torch alight."

He took some more snow from the shield, heated it up, wrung out the rag and continued.

"You have no infected wounds. You're lucky."

He grabbed her shoulders and turned her around. The large slanted eyes emanated a strange light. The girl may have looked bewildered, but there was so much more inside her— Hansio was sure of it. There was perhaps more than the Hero had ever seen in any human being.

Was it something more she had, or did she possess something that others did not?

Worry furrowed his brow, the lines transforming into a severe frown.

"I was sick and I had a bad dream," he began. "You were also in that dream. You made it less brutal. Before I lost my senses, I was convinced I would die."

The child's expression remained blank and unreadable. She

did not smile or even look saddened.

They stared at each other. Hansio felt his eyes sting and he turned to look at the Hastur sword. It was dirty, emanating the same blue light as before. Part of the blade was still clean and it allowed him to see his own reflection. His face appeared contorted and he could just see one eye. It was bloodshot like those of the living dead, and there were a few red tear drops under the skin. Thousands of crimson darts branched out from the yellow center of his iris.

He had once seen a painting by an artist of the Dying Lands. It was an imaginary portrayal of how the sun had been when it was in full vigor. The artist depicted a yellow sphere with numerous red lightning bolts that vanished into the cosmos. He pressed two fingers against his eye.

"Now, wrap yourself up in the fur and dry yourself next to the fire."

The child did not move, so Hansio got up and covered her up himself.

* * * *

Night had fallen and Hansio decided it would be wise to barricade the entrance. He took some of the bulkier funeral objects from the tomb and arranged them in front of the broken-down door.

If the living dead try to enter, at least they will not be able to do it without making a noise, he reasoned.

He gave the horse a cracker and caressed its face.

"You kept the little one warm with your breath. Thank you."

He returned to the fire and sat down. The girl's gaze was upon him and again, it was as if he could feel the weight of those unfathomable eyes.

"Sleep now. If I feel strong enough, we will leave tomorrow."

The child merely stared at him. With a frown, Hansio let out a deep sigh.

"My sword is a special weapon," he began in a soft but

uncertain tone, as if he was going to tell a fairy-tale. "It was forged by the Hastur and its creation is a legend. The fire of the forge is the hottest that exists in the Dying Lands and it is said that no human can resist such heat. The bellows work incessantly and the light is so bright that it can blind you. It is at these temperatures that this metal can be softened and worked."

Hansio raised the sword and pointed it towards the girl. For the first time, he felt he had captivated her with his words. "There is no hammer that can beat or deform this metal. No hammer is strong enough. In fact, the Hastur use what they call the magic of the gods. The metal levitates in the air of its own accord and the hands of the Hastur begin their work. They are the only ones who can resist that heat and the scorching metal cannot burn their skin. The steel stretches between their fingers, creating long, shiny, incandescent strands of light. Suspended as if upon an invisible loom, the threads are then woven into a thick steel fiber, like a rope." The child's body slid down until she was lying on her back, hands joined beneath her head.

"At this stage, the steel rope can be placed on an anvil and, using special magic, beaten like any other sword. However, once the blade has been modeled, it is not immersed in normal water, but inside a liquid that is colder than snow, a liquid that only magical jars, covered in ice, can hold."

The girl had fallen asleep with the doll beside her.

Hansio continued to gaze at his blue blade in a way he had not done for some time. It was something he had done perhaps once before—on the day he became a Hero. On that day he made his oath and received the sword and he regarded it with the eyes of someone in love.

As he gazed at the blade, he caught a glimpse of another part of his face. His beard was covered in earth and the blood and pus that had wept from his neck and eyes.

He exhaled heavily, again confused as to how he managed to avoid death and transformation. Then he took a handful of snow
from the large shield and placed it on his wound. He tried to wash it, but the friction made the pain even worse. This was not the pleasurable sensation from his dream.
Suddenly exhausted, he abandoned himself to sleep.

Chapter Nine

The line of the horizon was a wall of water, the frozen and perennially restless tides of the Gray Sea. Waves crashed against the rocky barricade of the tall cliffs, which seemed to come alive, breathing with every impact.

Marine birds had built their nests in the crevices, the pale sunset illuminating their damp feathers. They hovered just above the surface of the stormy sea, sprayed by the foam generated by the waves' impact with the rocks. Farther out, the crests of the undulating waters looked like the ferocious jaws of the creatures that inhabited its depths, leaping out as if trying to snap at the heedless birds.

The sounds of the waves rose upwards, higher than the salty spray, reaching a soft brittle meadow at the top of the cliffs that ended abruptly at a precipice.

The body of a man, a knight without a helmet and wearing fine chainmail, lay close to the verge, his hand reaching out into the emptiness. Perhaps he had intended to throw himself off the edge but died before reaching it. All of a sudden the ground beneath him trembled, shifting by a few inches, before settling down again. Then it collapsed completely, dragging the corpse with it. The Gray Sea devoured both earth and flesh.

A short distance from the cliffs rose a gray castle with a tower. On the ground before it lay a partially devoured body, waiting for purification or a new life as a creature hungry for human flesh. There were also many heads that had been broken or severed from their necks.

Everything seemed calm and night was falling. Nothing and no one moved, except a ripped garment, blown by the biting wind. Livid clouds threatened rain.

Someone inside the castle was still alive.

He was covered in the blood of his soldiers and the many

people he had been unable to save. A gory streak of brain matter stained his leg. Some of the blood was also his own. Hansio closed the heavy doorway with a wooden beam. He examined the clots on his leg and thought of the soldier whose skull he had smashed to prevent him returning from the dead. He cleaned himself with the sheath of his sword, then dropped it to the ground. Finally he had time to look around him. Someone had overturned some chairs and tables, perhaps in an attempt to barricade themselves inside while waiting for help. Evidently, they had not succeeded, given that the room was empty. There was evidence someone had been killed. There was blood everywhere, curtains and tapestries had been reduced to shreds and many torches abandoned on the floor. Only three or four remained lit. The Hero of the Dying Lands was exhausted, but still held his Hastur sword firmly in his grasp. His hands bore the signs of hand-to-hand combat. He had fought for hours and was gasping for breath. He had run, crawled and broken bones. The weapon glowed blue. One of the living dead was nearby. He moved forward a couple of paces and after abandoning his sheath he also abandoned the sword. The hall echoed with the sound of metal against the marble floor.

Hansio approached the body of his wife, abandoned on a large table. Something snapped inside of him. He straightened her out and arranged her as if she slept, looking up at the sky, one arm alongside her body and the other on her chest. Then he lay down beside her.

They finally found peace after the long day of bloodshed. Her lips were pale, there was a large bruise on her forehead and her hair was disheveled.

She was still incredibly beautiful even in death.

Hansio followed every curve of her face with his yellow eyes and, instinctively, he kissed her. She was still warm and soft. He kissed her again and reached his hand downwards, delicately caressing her between her legs. He kissed her on her neck, where he still smelled her perfume, mingled with the scent of blood. He wondered briefly whose blood it was and whether it was hers. It did not matter. Not anymore. He was excited and in love. His heart beat like the very first time they met. He was about to do something he knew society would not understand. It was something he found exceptionally beautiful, new, and strange. Lifting her skirt, he made love to her. He could not wait for her body to go cold. She would soon start to transform. It did not matter that the blood and innards were coming out of her abdomen with each thrust. Her limbs were lacerated, where they tore her skin with their nails and teeth.

Hansio could still hear her cry of terror as the creature bent over to devour her. The harrowing sounds were closely followed in Hansio's tortured mind by the terrible images. He stopped and hit the table with his fists to block out that momentary instant of horror. This was not the time to dwell on these monstrosities, he wanted to love her for the last time, say his last irrational goodbye, and nothing could pollute the beauty of this moment.

He felt good when he finished. To Hansio's mind, in his own twisted way, he had done something incredible, he demonstrated his love for her for the last time and said good-bye to her sweetly.

He abandoned himself on the table beside her, his weariness suddenly increasing a hundredfold. He embraced her and fell asleep as he had done a thousand times in their bed.

* * * *

A monstrous cry and the suffocating smell of death awoke him. He opened his eyes and found her still lying next to him. She had not transformed yet. He could not have been asleep long because her body was still slightly warm. It was now dark outside and the only sound was the icy sea wind that blew through the corridors of the castle with a sinister wail. Hansio thought of the lamenting souls of the people who died in the last few hours. He wondered then about the soul of his wife. Where was she now?

Without taking his yellow eyes off her still body, the Hero got down from the table and took two steps backwards.

Addressing her gently, he asked, "Is your voice among those that run through these corridors?"

For the first time, his bleak mind considered the darkest of possibilities. It was a heresy the Hastur would have fiercely condemned.

Human beings don't have a soul.

The thought was torment, and as it penetrated his consciousness, another terrifying noise came from the hall, echoing from somewhere behind him. He ignored it for now, his mind still focused on his wife and another painful task he must carry out.

Her head was drooping and he moved back to the table. He placed a hand on his sword and another on his wife's knee. Caressing her, he then immersed his hands into her open belly.

His gestures were slow and confident, as if he had meditated on what to do for some time, although in reality he was merely following his instincts. He stretched out the wound and pulled something small and bloody from her body, a fetus, a minuscule human being, still not completely formed. He laid it reverently next to its mother, in the place where he had been sleeping just a moment before. The child would have been born in the south, as far away from the Frontier as possible, which would have allowed it to be born alive. Circumstances had intervened, he thought bitterly.

Somewhere behind him came another inhuman sound and this time Hansio's brain interpreted the horrendous noise. He froze without turning. A heavy veil fell over him and again the thought returned.

No living being has a soul.

It sent shivers through his very core.

He pulled out his dagger, which he kept tied to his calf and cut what remained of his wife's clothing. Her breast was soft and pale and it was not difficult to remove. It would have given rancid milk near the Frontier. He weighed it in his hand and observed it morbidly under the faint light of the torch, blood dripping from his fingers. Then he secured his dagger under his belt.

Again he heard the frightful cry. It sounded like the growl of a hungry animal and, as if incited by it, he bit into the lump of flesh in his hand. He tore a sliver and chewed it without feeling disgust. It bore no flavor for him.

A wild, chilling cry echoed his gesture.

Hansio swallowed the morsel.

The Hero's eyes became ferocious and finally he turned. Tied to two iron hooks on the wall was a living corpse. With an intelligence limited to a few animalistic instincts, purely to satisfy its incessant hunger, it was not bothered by the ropes that bound it to the wall. One was wrapped around its neck, while another two bound each wrist, but it walked towards Hansio seemingly oblivious.

The Hero moved towards it with the dripping breast in his hand and noticed its attention was focused on the piece of meat.

"Once you were a man," he said. "The coat of arms on your tattered clothes shows you lived in the East a hundred years ago. Those lands were infested a century ago and your home is now many leagues beyond the Frontier."

The creature was hungry and Hansio knew it did not understand. Nevertheless, he continued, as if he could convince it of its essential humanity.

"You were once a knight of the East, one of the valorous

warriors whose deeds are still sung today. Now, you are nothing."

The being snarled and grunted, drooling from its mouth. Its odor, the smell of rotting flesh, was suffocating.

"Is this what you want?" he held what remained of the truncated breast towards it. "Is this what you wanted? You tasted it when you ripped open her body and I did too, because this flesh belonged to me. Now it is nothing more but food for the worms or for you damned beings."

Hansio grabbed the creature abruptly by the throat. It moaned but did not take its eyes off the succulent morsel.

"If I gave you this piece of my wife, what would you do?" Hansio cried.

"Would you go to her there on the table or would you come to me? My flesh is fresher than this."

He raised the breast above the creature's head. Its teeth gnashed in an attempt to bite even just a tiny piece. Hansio clenched his fist and the last drops of blood fell on the monster's face, directly into its mouth.

"You're hungry, you're always hungry. Here, have it. Eat!" Hansio dropped the meat to the floor and released his grip on its neck. The being pounced on the flesh and devoured it under the yellow, angry eyes of the Hero. He watched as the creature ate and then without a sound or warning, slipped his knife from his belt and drove it through its skull. The metal point of the blade came out from under its chin. A piece of chewed breast dropped from its mouth. Hansio regarded it without emotion.

He slumped to the floor cross-legged, lost, catatonic. All reason slipped away from him.

A barrage of violent blows shattered the momentary peace and shook the doors of the hall. It was enough to force the doors to cave in, but Hansio remained as he was, his mind elsewhere. Splinters of wood flew into the hall and another blow brought the blade of a double-headed axe striking through.

It took just several more blows for an imposing warrior, a Hero whose sword shone like Hansio's, to enter the hall with a Hastur closely behind him.

Hansio recognized Martos. He regarded the scene before him with an expression of disgust. His eyes filled with anxiety and then urgency.

"Soon there will be an invasion," he said. "The Hooded Ones are just a short distance from here," he added.

"You have come too late," Hansio replied.

Sheathing his axe, Martos bowed his head in assent.

"We have arrived late, I know. Your lands are lost and even if they weren't I have not seen any of the inhabitants left alive."

Hansio stared at him.

"The Frontier continues to retreat. My lands, my people are lost—and not just them."

Martos was resolute. "The Resistance will continue until the day the Ark is ready!"

It sounded like a battle cry.

Hansio did not hear his determined words. In his mind floated the still-terrifying thought, Not one of us has a soul...

"We must go," interrupted Martos.

Hansio did not move and Martos was forced to lift him to his feet.

Forcing Hansio to look him in the eye, he said, slowly, "You are still a Hero. You have an oath to respect."

The Hastur grabbed Hansio by the arm and led him outside. His will was lost, and his head drooped.

Martos looked over at the severed body of the woman. He noticed the fetus on the table and her slashed belly, and cast an incredulous gaze at Hansio. Maintaining his cool composure, he placed his hand on the hilt of his Hastur sword, raised it high and cut off her head with one swift blow. Hansio, his back turned, heard every sound, even the thud of her head as it fell to the floor. He felt nothing.

Chapter Ten

Hansio awoke feeling emotionally numb; his only sensation the physical pain.

The child slept and the fire was out. It was cold but the tomb retained the heat quite well. He needed to check the weather, to determine whether they could continue their journey.

After moving the barricade of objects from the doorway, he clambered up the mound towards the fresh air and daylight. As a precaution, he took his sword with him. He raised his face to the sky. It was clear and the sallow, newly-risen sun was low. The conditions seemed perfect. The daylight still irritated his eyes.

To make his descent easier, he searched for the footprints he left during the climb. Suddenly, out of the corner of his eye, he saw a shadow move behind a nearby tomb. He clenched his teeth and dived to his knees, hiding in the snow. The Hastur sword shone a bright blue and Hansio recognized a solitary cadaver stumbling towards him. The monster had definitely picked up the scent of living flesh and was following it. It would not take it long to find them.

Hansio observed it from his hiding place and noticed it was struggling to move in the snow. It would walk a few paces, fall, get back up then fall again. Despite the obvious difficulties, it was clear it was on the right track. Hansio crouched further down in the snow, trying to think. The creature would definitely find them, so he might as well get there first, face it head on and shorten the wait.

He knew he was not ready to fight. The wound on his neck hampered his movements and the poison from the Hooded One was still in his bloodstream. Only one enemy lay before him and it was clearly at a disadvantage, struggling to move across the difficult terrain.

Hansio gripped the Hastur sword and took two large strides

into the open, sliding down the side of the mound on the snow. He cleared the white flakes from his face and realized the creature had already spotted him. It gave its typical cry and gnashed its teeth, moving like a crazed, awkward animal. After a few paces, Hansio already felt tired and his labored breathing came in short pants, condensing and rising above him in thick clouds.

He took two more difficult steps forward and watched as the creature collapsed in the snow. Hansio stopped. It would take nothing to smash its skull, but he decided to wait and catch his breath. There would be another easy opportunity when he felt slightly stronger. He swallowed, breathed out and looked at the sun.

The living corpse snarled, got back on its feet, stretched out a hand and opened its mouth. It was monstrous, just like all the others.

Hansio raised his sword and prepared to strike. They were now just a few paces away from each other.

As well as the crunch of trampled snow, he now heard the coldblooded growl of the creature and the sound of his own gasping breath. The tip of his sword pointed to the sky. Hansio waited, his pose ungainly, like someone holding a sword for the first time. His arms were raised, his legs astride.

He looked the creature straight in the eye, the vile image reminding him briefly of his own reflection in the blade. Hansio brought his sword down violently, but an uncharacteristic moment of indecision made him swerve the blow. Instead of splitting its head in two, he struck its shoulder, chopping off an arm. The creature fell backwards. Hansio stood immobile.

He could not explain what caused him to change aim at the last minute.

Confused, Hansio waited for the target to come for him

again, but the monster was having difficulty getting up. Taking advantage of the creature's unsteadiness, he moved in this time for what would surely be the deathblow. He raised his sword and stepped forward, finding the bleeding gaze of the being behind a mound of snow. Yet again he felt uncertain. Something else troubled him, something more than those red, bloodshot eyes. There was something familiar in its face. Despite the transformation the creature still possessed physical traits of the man he had once been. A slow, dark stream of blood soiled the icy candor.

Hansio pulled away abruptly to avoid the grip of the other hand jerkily moving towards him. He raised his sword more decisively this time and hacked off the other arm, just below the elbow. The forearm and hand flew far away, leaving a splatter of tiny, crimson drops across the snow.

Hansio stood and observed the monster as it rolled inside the snowy hole, drenched in the fluid that gushed from its truncated limbs. He was disgusted by the scene, but he had not finished with him yet. Whatever his hesitation before, there was no pity now.

He leaned over and grabbed the beast by the throat, narrowly avoiding a bite. He punched it in the face with the hilt of his sword, loosening several teeth, making it appear even less threatening. He lowered his head and again scrutinized the familiar face carefully. Then, brusquely, he pushed the creature back, grabbed it by the ankle and dragged it into his hiding place.

Hansio threw the beast to the ground, face down, directly in front of the sarcophagus. With one foot on the nape of its neck, he immobilized it by tying a rope around its neck and attaching the other end around its ankles, forcing it into an arched position. The creature struggled uselessly, reminding him of a wriggling worm.

Leaving it for now, and satisfied that it could pose no threat, the Hero sat down next to the still warm embers of the fire. The little girl was on her knees, on the other side of the chamber, staring at the prey he had brought in. Hansio had not considered the effect the living corpse would have on the child. While she did not take her eyes off it, she did not seem perturbed by the furious movements or chilling sounds.

The wounded warrior studied his prey and suddenly realized why the shriveled face looked so familiar. This man had been part of his militia. He had fought with him. He should have recognized him by his clothes, but they were too threadbare and dirty. The soldier had also courageously defended the castle during the last attack. This was why Hansio had hesitated to make the final blow. He had lost his life in vain. Hansio wondered again why he had not, like the soldier, been transformed. He shifted his gaze from his old companion in arms to the child. She was still tense and on her knees, her huge eyes fixed on the monster.

The Hero spoke to the creature. "Do you recognize me?"

He waited, but the being was thrashing on the ground and a dark liquid oozed from the stumps of its arms and mouth. Hansio got up and held its head firmly to stop it from moving, forcing it to look him in the eye.

"Do you remember who you are?" he asked. "Who you were? Can you remember your life before you changed?"

His fingers gripped the cold, hard cheeks but there was no reply.

Undeterred, Hansio continued, "We fought together to defend the Dying Lands. We feasted together to celebrate our victories with the little fruits that our lands gave us. We were proud of our battles. We were proud to represent the Resistance on the shores of the Gray Sea. Do you remember the stormy sea? Do you remember?"

Gradually, Hansio filled with rage as his interrogation was met with silence. Then he was calm.

"No, of course not." He shook his head. "You're dead." He sat back down next to the embers, the effort making him weary. "You exist merely to satisfy your hunger. You cannot remember when we still believed in the soul, when we still believed in the Ark."

Suddenly the child moved her head and fixed her huge eyes upon him.

The gaze was the same, lost and innocuous, but there was something about the slanted eyes which was beginning to irritate him. It was as if they saw something he could not, that they knew something about him and the world around them of which he was unaware.

Suddenly, it dawned on him that he had not been trying to convince the creature of the existence of the soul or the existence of the Ark. He had been trying to convince himself. The realization was unbearable. The discomfort it aroused was so strong that he rose to his feet gritting his teeth, looking for his dagger.

He marched over to the living corpse, and plunged the dagger into its temple. The creature immediately stopped writhing.

Hansio stood and contemplated the results of his actions, but he could still feel the girl's gaze upon him. Like a judge, or a conscience.

He let go of the dagger and sat back down. The child retreated under her fur, averting her penetrating stare. Hansio could not tell if she had gone back to sleep.

On one side there was anger, hunger and the past. On the other there was what the Hastur defined as the future—hope. He did not believe in a future, or hope. Even if it was obvious that the child concealed a great secret, it was not a secret Hansio was desperate to find out.

* * * *

Hansio prepared his things to leave.

He retrieved his rope and dagger and threw what remained of the creature in a heap against the wall.

The route outside had already been cleared. Now, all he needed to do was open up a passage for the stallion.

He dug hurriedly with the shield, but it took longer than he hoped because his wounds still pained him.

Instinct was telling him to hurry. Hansio felt the tension growing in his breast. When he finished, with the snow up to his ankles and his back towards the Valley of Tombs, he noticed a glow from the sheath of his sword, which lay a short distance away on the ground. In an instant, he realized it was not merely a glow but an intense blue light. His heart skipped a beat. He turned abruptly, clutching the edge of the shield.

How could I have been so foolish? he scolded himself in astonishment.

He was surrounded by more living dead than he could have counted in a single glance. There were hordes of them and they were everywhere, standing just thirty paces away. There was no escape.

He heard a cry of hunger and the sound of rapid footsteps in the snow. Something came from the right and grabbed him by the hair. Hansio felt his back bow and a sharp pain from his wound, but his reflexes were primed. With a jerk of his shoulder, he managed to keep the enemy at a distance, pushing the beast away with his hands. A lock of his hair caught beneath the black nails of the attacker. Without hesitation, Hansio hit the monster with the edge of his shield. He did not succeed in decapitating it, but managed to open a wound just below its eye, deep enough to reach its brain. The being slumped to the ground, the shield lodged in its body. Hansio swiftly assessed the situation. His breath came fast and he realized that the only way to survive would be to return inside the tomb and defend himself to the end.

Behind a group of living dead, he caught sight of one of the Hooded Ones. He was probably not alone. Hansio ran inside to retrieve his sword and quickly barricaded the doorway once more.

Strategically, he was in a good position. Anyone who entered would be forced to follow a tortuous path. Furthermore, he could face the enemy without having to watch his back.

He wondered aloud how long he could last and how many there would be.

He was not afraid. Hansio knew how to control his fear. This was a cold and realistic calculation—there were far too many of them.

He observed the light that came from outside, unsheathed his sword and stood on guard. His body was twisted at an awkward angle, making his neck hurt.

Wrapped in the fur, the child appeared behind him clutching the doll in her hands. Hansio softened and lowered his sword, for an instant forgetting the incumbent enemy.

If—or when—he gave in, he knew the child would also die.

He noticed the child's hands clutching the fur and the tattered clothes of the doll. The fur had slipped down onto her arm, exposing her shoulder. The bones pressed against her skin, making her look fragile and defenseless.

The sight of her fragility was all Hansio needed to restore his strength and determination. Yes, she would die—but only if he gave in first.

He drew the dagger from his belt, and slid it across the floor to the child's bare feet.

"Take it," he said. He opened his mouth to give her further instructions, but stopped.

Those eyes were too naive and innocent and she was too little to understand what that gesture meant. If anything happened to him, the wisest thing to do would be to use the dagger on herself.

She did not understand. The handle hit her foot, but she did not pick it up.

Pointing to the room containing the sarcophagus, he shouted, "Go inside!"

In that instant came the crash of splintered wood and more furious cries. The girl retreated to the chamber, the dagger still on the floor.

The first creatures hurled the funeral objects aside. Hansio counted a dozen or so, advancing in line, some side by side where the passageway allowed.

The Hero took a step forward.

His muscles were swollen and ready to fight, his mind trying to ignore the pain of his old wounds.

The first creature was just a step away when the Hastur sword moved swiftly. The creature's head rolled to one side along with a piece of skull and the brain matter from the next in line. Hansio regarded his first two victims, recalling how he had escaped the assault in the village. He had taken advantage of the bodies on the ground to slow down their advancement. This time, he again found himself in a narrow space. The tactic would be the same, he decided—the only difference was that this time there was no escape route behind him.

The air whistled and with a single movement two more fell, another immediately appearing behind them. Hansio took a step backwards to gain some room for wielding his sword. He swore between his teeth and split the head of his enemy in two.

I'm already retreating, he thought, angrily.

He considered using the opportunity to advance, but the number of opponents was so great it would have been a foolish move. He turned to check how much space there was between the entrance and the sarcophagus. The unexpected movement in his neck made his body sway.

Hansio raised his sword and pointed it out in front of him for protection, waiting for the wave of pain to pass.

Pain will bring suffering only if you fear it. It is a sensation like any other. It all depends on your mind.

Hansio had never thought of those words before, although they came to him as familiarly as if he had spoken them every day.

They were the words cited by the Heroes when pain overwhelmed them, part of the Heroes' Oath.

Martos would certainly have thought of those words before he died.

Pain does not exist when you are fighting for the gods.

The memories floored him, and Hansio's knee gave way.

Is that really what I swore?he wondered, astonished.

His wrist weakened and gave way under the weight of the blade.

In front of him, the advance of the ravenous men, women and children continued. The first wave tripped over the beheaded bodies and fell, just as Hansio had hoped. The Hero used the moment to recover himself and strengthen his legs. He stepped back, took two deep breaths and continued with the necessary onslaught. He smashed the head of a dead woman who was trying to get back on her feet and chopped off a hand that grabbed his ankle. He twirled his sword above his head and the tip clinked against the wall. The point brushed the rocky walls of the tomb, producing a yellow spark which contrasted starkly with the blue light of the blade, briefly illuminating the gloom.

He lowered the sword again, but each blow was becoming weaker than the last. Without realizing, he was now almost on the threshold of the burial chamber. He spotted the dagger on the ground and swiftly retrieved it.

The sea of living dead had slowed but showed no signs of stopping. He gripped the dagger and drove it into the head of a dead boy, then hit the mouth of another man who came too close, smashing his teeth in.

...when you fight for the gods...pain...only if you fear it...

Certain words ran over and over in his mind, like a melody of a song or the ecstatic, repetitive chant of a prayer.

The walls and floor of the corridor were now covered with dark blood and brain matter, the Hastur sword illuminating the horror with its blue light. The cries of rage and suffering that rebounded from one side of the room to the other were his own, but they were echoed by the inhuman cries of the living dead.

Hansio caught sight of the child. She was waiting just inside the door of the funeral chamber, wrapped in the fur, still with wide uncomprehending eyes.

I want to take you with me, he thought, staring at her innocent face.

I want to be able to protect you. Death is the best protection from transformation and this dying world. I want to be inside that sarcophagus, holding your fragile bones.

The thought held a flavor of the life he led before he became a wandering warrior of the Frontier. Until that time he had no idea that life had a flavor. This way of life had become so normal that he could hardly recognize it. In that moment he realized he had never before thought of holding someone's bones or sharing such an intimate desire for absolute peace with another.

Hansio was disturbed. He had forgotten that such feelings could even exist. The image was morbid and terrifying.

Lost as he was in this rapid chain of thought, the sword still moved, almost of its own accord, saving him from two aggressors. Without warning, a memory re-emerged-a memory which gave him renewed strength and something startlingly akin to hope.

The tombs were all connected.

The memory sprung from words spoken by the Hasturs, words he had forgotten.

"The souls of the deceased warriors and kings would leave their bodies to reunite with their ancestors and teach the living to understand the language of the gods."

Hansio had long-since dismissed this. He had stopped believing in the soul.

He twirled his sword with skill, causing three of the creatures to fall on top of each other. A mass of five or six bodies formed, giving him time to make a run for the burial chamber.

He took the child in his arms and grabbed the saddle bag in the other. He glanced at his horse, sensing its agitation.

Hansio closed his eyes and quickly visualized where he had seen the sun in the sky. He orientated himself and identified the rout west. The passageway that would lead him to safety must be behind the western wall of the burial chamber. He shoved the horse with his shoulder to move it closer to the wall.

He found it straight away. The entrance to the connecting passage was beneath an ancient inscription, "The soul cannot die, it remains as light, in memory of what was and what humankind will become."

"We're getting out of here," he told the stallion. Although his tone was urgent, it also betrayed his worry and hinted at an underlying sadness.

The furious cries at the entrance of the corridor multiplied. Time was running out.

Hansio put the girl and the sack down and touched the wall of rock. His fingers found a small fissure.

Hastur magic cuts stone perfectly, he thought, unsurprised their skillful craft hid the opening in the rocks so well.

He cast a gentle glance at the horse behind him.

They were in a hurry and he was acting on impulse. He

aimed his sword and drove it into the almost invisible slit. The sword entered easily and the rock parted. The Hastur's magic had done its work. A dark tunnel opened out before him.

An ancient air current tousled his hair, brushing the skin of his face. He pushed the girl into the tunnel first, then turned to his horse. A tear slid down his cheek.

Until then, he did not know what tears were.

The first of the living dead broke into the burial chamber, its hunger relentless.

With the fury of just one fist, he smashed its head.

Right now, he only had a heart and eyes for his horse.

Using his dagger, he cut a lock of its mane and held it in his fist.

The stallion kicked out suddenly, breaking the head of a female creature. Hansio kissed him between the eyes and led him delicately towards the entrance of the tunnel.

Then he let go. He could not find any words. Hansio cut the horse's throat.

The animal tried to whinny, but all it could muster was a gurgle. It kicked out and the sound of breaking bones and the furious cries of inhuman beings filled the small chamber.

Hansio turned his back on his trusted beast and picked up the girl and his sack. He felt the hot spray of the animal's blood splattered across his face.

His head and shoulders brushed against the walls of the tunnel. The proud stallion would never have been able to pass through such a tight passage.

Hansio thought he heard the animal one last time and silently thanked him for the time he gave them by sacrificing his own life.

Chapter Eleven

The Hastur sword illuminated the dark tunnel. It was the only source of light—in his haste, Hansio had forgotten to take the torch.

A wound had opened in his chest that was bigger and much more painful than the others. This was the type of wound that only time can heal. He had not experienced pain like this since the day his wife died. During all those years wandering the Frontier, in the grip of his burning desire for a cull, he had not truly been alone. At his side had been his trusty steed. Now all that remained of his constant companion was a lock of hair wrapped around his fingers.

The pain that should not be feared in the oath of the Heroes was physical in nature. Right now, Hansio knew he was incapable of withstanding any other form of agony.

The flesh of his wife ended up between the jaws of the living dead. The torment was so great it was intolerable. Yes, Hansio thought, the only pain he could bear was physical. Filled with grief at the memory, he wondered whether he had become stronger or more vulnerable since that day. It was a question he could not answer-one of far too many which surfaced these days.

The cries of the living dead grew weaker, but Hansio knew there was no more time to stop. They would have gorged themselves on the meat of the horse but they would come again—for him and for the child.

The tight passageway led into a slightly wider tunnel. It seemed to head in the same direction and Hansio proceeded without hesitation. There had been no corners or deviations and they appeared to be going in a straight line. He could barely feel the weight of the girl in his arms, but thoughts of his horse and its cruel fate weighed heavily on his back. They advanced quickly, the sword light still glowing strong, as if it were warning them to find a way out as quickly as possible.

All of a sudden the echoes of his footsteps grew silent. The blue light filtered upwards, and the ceiling vanished into obscurity. Even the air was different.

For the first time, Hansio slowed down and looked around him. He had come to the end of the tunnel and was now in a much larger chamber. It was so dark, Hansio could not guess its size, but the ceiling was much higher than that of the tunnel and the light from the sword could not reach it. He put the girl down on the ground and took her hand. Hansio could have held at least three hands like hers in his. She was so delicate he could easily have crushed her bones. He gripped her firmly but gently so he would not lose her in the dark.

He moved into what he assumed was the center of the room, but soon realized the sword light only lit up a small area and that, if he continued onwards, he would lose all sense of direction. Before it was too late, he decided to retrace his steps. He was about to turn when he caught sight of a bulky shape in the darkness. Curious, he walked towards it.

He arrived at a circular altar, which was so large he could see only a small part of it. He let go of the girl's hand and touched it. It was the same rough stone of the sarcophagus they had just abandoned. This is where the living met with the ancient souls.

The counsel of the great men buried in these tombs would be helpful right now, he thought.

"Where are you?" he cried, angrily. "Where are your souls?" He clenched his teeth and, for a moment, it felt as if an answer might come from the darkness. There was nothing.

There was no time to waste. He scooped up the girl and retraced his steps, quickly reaching the opening of the tunnel. Then, some distance away, he spotted another, identical passageway. Yet another tunnel opened up directly next to it. He swore between his teeth, hoping with all his heart that he was not lost. He looked at the ground. He could not risk taking a path that would lead him closer to the living dead.

Thinking fast, he looked down again and found his own footprints impressed in a thick layer of dust. This reassured him. Now he could find the tunnel they had just left and get his bearings again. Then, he had been convinced he was heading west. If he wanted to get as far away as possible from the living dead, he would need to find another tunnel, possibly heading north or east. Having identified the tunnel they had used before, he walked to the right, following the circular wall of the hall, passing numerous tunnels as he went. They were all the same. He chose one instinctively. He was certain it would lead him to another tomb. After several strides into the darkness, he once again heard the muffled cries of the living dead. They were so faint he thought it might be his imagination. As they continued, Hansio became more and more convinced they must be real—and that the creatures had already reached the large hall.

Hansio quickened his pace and reached again what appeared to be a dead end. He searched the wall in front of him with his hands and found the hidden slit, placed the tip of his blade in the opening and pushed. The Hastur's magic did the rest. As the passageway opened, Hansio hoped there were no living dead on the other side. If there were, it would be the end.

All he found on the other side was darkness.

Moving swiftly forward, the sword lit up a new sarcophagus. There was no time to pause over the inscriptions or the funeral objects in the tomb. Briefly, he considered whether there might be something of use. No. All he needed was his sword and the contents of his saddle bag.

He soon found the ancient doorway to the tomb. He let go of the child, took his sword and began striking the wood with furious, exhausting blows. Finally, he managed to break through, but no light came through the hole. Frustrated, Hansio leaned on his sword to get his breath back. The oozing gash in his neck throbbed painfully. Then, in the pause between two breaths, an entire mountain of snow poured through the entrance. The door of this tomb had also been blocked by a deep drift. There could not be much distance between them and the surface.

He carefully created an opening with his hands, trying to avoid being buried alive. A hand suddenly scratched at the air, before his weak eyes were wounded by the light of the dying sun.

Hansio took his sack and threw it outside. He waited. There was no sound, but the Hastur sword was still glowing. This was not a good sign. The living dead were still too close by. He widened the hole in the snow so he could put his head out and assess the situation.

All he could see was pure white. An initial furtive glance told him there were not even any footprints. His view was obstructed when a wall of the passageway suddenly collapsed. Hansio decided to let the girl out first then quickly extract himself. He had to move cautiously because he also ran the risk of getting trapped.

He pushed the child out and then sank his feet into the snow, climbing through the passage until his torso was out the other side. He placed a knee on the edge, but felt it give way as the snow suddenly caved in. His knee sank deep into the snow. Hansio's leg was trapped. Immediately, he checked left and right to see if the living dead had reached them, but it appeared as if time was on their side—they still had not picked up their scent. He leaned his hands on the snow, but his limbs sank further, his body slipping downwards by several inches. He would have to emerge gradually, without making any sudden movements. It was a slow and painstaking progress, but eventually he emerged. He pushed the girl away from the hole and picked up his sack.

He looked up, finding the sun, pale and dying in the sky, as it always was. Why did he feel it was different just a moment before? The wound at the death of his horse throbbed again, causing far more pain than the one on his neck.

He lowered his gaze, feeling the tiny hand of the girl as it vanished inside his large palm. Hansio found it hard to look into those enormous slanted eyes, which seemed to read his every thought.

The sun was dying and he wondered when his turn would finally come.

Turning to the child, he exclaimed bitterly, "The souls of the dead were not a light for us down there!"

He clenched his teeth with anger, seeing the inscription on the tomb before him. Then he pushed away his dark thoughts and resolved to continue their journey. Hansio calculated they must have travelled either north or east below ground.

"The river," he said. "We were looking for the river when we escaped the village. We have to find it to return to the Frontier in the south. I don't want to get lost again. If another blizzard arrives..." He paused, again trying to dismiss his most troubling thoughts.

"The river meets the Valley of Tombs to the north-east. It's a long way round, but it doesn't matter."

As they proceeded through the white sea of foul-smelling snow, Hansio used the sun to navigate their path and adjusted his direction. The light of the sword diminished, almost going out completely.

* * * *

Night fell and they were fortunate to meet the river before they were enveloped in total darkness. The snow was not as deep and walking was less tiresome. Every now and then they came across human footprints, but they were not to be fooled, the living dead were everywhere. No human being could survive far from the Frontier.

Hansio did not want to light a fire, for fear of attracting attention, but he found a recess by the shallows of the river where they could shelter and rest. They shared a Hastur cracker and lay down in each other's arms.

Once he was settled, Hansio's thoughts returned to the horse. He had forgotten to hide him. He jumped up, but stopped himself. He would no longer need to worry about the stallion. His frustration made him long to scream out loud. Even the human tendency to affection had become his enemy.

The Hero fell into a troubled sleep, but like all warriors he remained on guard.

* * * *

At dawn he continued on his way, keeping to the shores of the river. The dark, filthy water stank of death. For drinking water he preferred to gather and suck on handfuls of snow. He was cold and weak and still tormented by physical and emotional pain. He must not forget they were still in the Infested Lands.

When the sun was at its halfway point in the sky, a memory surfaced from his childhood. These lands near the Gray Sea, the lands of his ancestors, had always belonged to him and now, walking through them again, he remembered a place that had once been special to him.

When he was young he had been taught to fight the living dead, but he was also allowed to enjoy a few small pleasures—before the dead devoured everything he owned. Without a word, he took the child in his arms and veered off

111

from the river. It was only a short detour and, when they reached the spot, Hansio gave a rare glimmer of a smile. Clouds of vapor rose from the ground into the sky, snorting like a raging animal. The jets were twice the height of a man and they were warm. Hansio made his way through the columns, until his feet were immersed in a foul-smelling, but hot spring.

He removed the fur from the child and plunged her into the dark gray water, washing her with the same gentleness he had used inside the tomb. The idea was to rest and get warm again. He bathed her quickly and then sat the child on a rock in the water while he removed his own clothes. His skin was still covered with what remained of the dry innards of the living dead he had rubbed on himself before entering the village days before.

Obscured by suffering, he abandoned all caution. The eyes of the girl were still upon him. He slipped into the torpid liquid of the spring, without letting the water touch the wound on his neck.

He closed his eyes and, as he had not done for far too long, relaxed every muscle in his body.

In that instant, even the noxious fumes of the waters seemed to disappear. A pleasurable shiver quivered through his body. Engrossed in the warmth, he wished he could stay there forever. He opened his eyes.

His yellow irises met with the light of the pallid sun, reminding him of death, of what he left behind and what awaited him and the child if they indulged themselves too long. He lowered his mouth to the water and took a small sip. The taste was rancid and made him feel sick. He would have liked to clean his wound before getting out, but decided against it. All he could do was enjoy the warmth of the water that came from deep below the ground. Hansio doubted staying there too long would be healthy. The Infested Lands, the Hooded Ones, their existence of death and putrefaction had even managed to corrupt the depths of earth too.

He did not immerse his head, but he rinsed his face and beard. The odor of the water would mingle with the air and the smell would soon go away.

He got out of the spring and, still naked, placed the gray fur around the slender shoulders of the girl, who rose carefully to avoid wetting it.

Their hair and clothes would never dry in the cold air of the Infested Lands.

* * * *

They walked for two days along the shore of the river, which slithered towards the east. Hansio was exhausted and in an attempt to regain his energies, imagined the water course beside him as it plunged off the rocks into the Gray Sea. A tall and immense waterfall, it was a breathtaking sight and a wonder of nature. It too was devoured by the Infested Lands. Although it was lost forever, the idea that the river could free itself from the claws and limitations of the territory at the end of its course gave him a sense of serenity.

Hansio lifted his gaze and searched for the dying sun. There it was again, as it had always been. He found relief in imagining the agony of the star as it reached the end of its days. Everything would end sooner or later.

During those days, they stumbled across a few stray, wandering cadavers and even a group of them, accompanying a Hooded One to an unknown destination. The Hero always tried to avoid a clash, but when that was impossible he had fought knowing he risked defeat.

Many a time, the rhythmic sound of the stallion's hooves echoed in his ears and he felt the sensation of his hand on its mane and face. Initially, he kept turning around to make sure the horse was following, but after a while he stopped. The deep snow gradually transformed into mud and sludge.

* * * *

On the night of the fourth day, Hansio awoke with a start.
They had found another refuge near the shore, under the
trunk of an ancient tree fallen many years before. The Hastur
blade glowed intensely and the sound of footsteps put him on
alert. They were too near to hope they had not picked up
their scent. There was more than one. The footsteps
suggested several were nearby. The Hero jumped to his feet
and unsheathed his sword.
Even though his eyes were used to the dark, the night was
impenetrable. He heard the grunt of hunger and realized it
was a pack of living dead...but he could not see them. They
were close, but not enough to see them with the light of his
sword. Their presence, the noises they made and the delay in
their attack concerned Hansio. They must be with a Hooded
One.
He was probably surrounded.
Hansio strained desperately to see in the dark. Nothing.
He closed his eyes and let his other senses be his guide. The
girl's breathing allowed him to locate her directly behind
him, almost curled up between his legs. The hungry growls of
the dead were difficult to place, because there were far too
many of them. There were at least a dozen, but he could not
be certain.
He was holding the sword too tightly in a grip which would
make his movements awkward. His hands were swollen with
cold and his stiff muscles made everything harder.
He adjusted his grip. The air whistled as the first aggressor
leapt upon him. Hansio twirled his sword and a head fell.
Immediately he heard another and then another, as if the
Hooded One had suddenly let his dogs off the leash.
There was no time to think.
Hansio imagined the blue glow as a sharp and purifying trail
that slashed at flesh, bone and darkness. He opened his eyes

and saw this was so.

The blue glow lit up his opponent just an instant before he struck and if he had believed in the gods, he would have thought a divine thunderbolt had come to his aid.

The sword is mine, he reminded himself. It is my hands that move.

Another blow left a blue trail in the air like the tail of a comet, splitting the head of the creature in two.

There was a pause in the attack—perhaps he had defeated them all... He heard a sound to his right and he moved quickly. It was not an attack. They were retreating. He held the sword in both hands and lashed out in the dark. The sword fell, striking at a diagonal, breaking open yet another skull.

Hansio listened to the night but did not hear any other noises. The blue light of the blade weakened.

He felt he had prolonged his life yet again. Another enemy had been vanquished.

The last skull belonged to the Hooded One.

After a while the sky clear and the dying sun rose in the east.

All around him were the hacked bodies of the creatures. Hansio did not stop to count them. He took the girl in his arms and continued on his way.

The Frontier could not be far.

Chapter Twelve

They walked along the river shore for another two days. The
wound on his neck still hurt and smelled foul, but Hansio
had become used to the torment. His yellow eyes, still tinged
with red, looked like the sun did on a summer day, or rather,
how the artists portrayed it in their frescoes. Hansio had
never known a real summer, only a succession of cold
seasons which barely changed and melted into one long
winter. The spring could be distinguished from the summer
only if you counted the days and the few rare buds on the
hardier plants.

Maybe his grandfather's grandfather had seen warmer times.
As he walked, Hansio focused on the annoying throb of his
flesh, or the color of his wound-covered limbs reflected in the
mirror-like surface of his sword. It was easier to concentrate
on his physical wounds rather than face the other, more
intense pain which throbbed deep in his breast.

His strength was leaving him and even the relatively light
weight of the child burdened him. He could no longer carry
her in his arms for great lengths of time. For long stretches
they would slow down and walk side by side, often hand in
hand, at other times separated by a single step.

The cold of the Infested Lands was penetrating. As soon as
they stopped to rest, the Hero felt as if his bones had been
covered in a layer of prickly crystals. The gray fur remained
wrapped tightly around the child's shoulders, however dirty
it had become.

At the start of his mission, he had never considered the
possibility of being so distant from the Frontier for such a
long time, far away from the mountains or villages where you
could get blankets and clothing. They were facing the
perennial winter of an agonizing world. He had never
imagined he would have to face the torments of the snow all

the way to the Valley of Tombs. In all that time, his mind had
even found a misty corner where he could pretend to forget
the horrors he had seen in his once so familiar homeland.
It was useless thinking he could have prepared better, or
brought more useful supplies.
Even one extra object would have been a hindrance. The
thoughts, which came one after another, helped him to block
out the darkest anguish in his mind.
Like a parasite that keeps a flesh wound open, Hansio was
aware that the memory of his wife was the fire that fueled all
his other mental agony.
He had attached the lock of the stallion's mane to a thin
piece of leather and tied it to the cross-shaped hand-guard of
his sword. His frost-bitten hands teased and smoothed the
hair continually. It was only when he was holding the child
that he stopped touching it obsessively. In his ears, he could
hear a distant hum, a cruel trick of the mind, reminding him
of the gurgling whinny of the animal. Its last cry had been
muffled by its own blood. Again his thoughts took flight.
He had been forced to abandon him.
He could not prevent Martos from decapitating his wife's
body.

* * * *

If only we were in a wood beyond the Frontier, then I could
hunt and find us some food. Hansio desperately steered his
mind onto more immediate concerns.
Even a fur. No-it's been years since there were animals in the
woods of the Frontier.
The woman he met just before Martos appeared suddenly
came to mind, the one with the sliver of hare's flesh between
her teeth.
I could skin one of the living dead and make some leather, he
thought.
No. It would take too long. The child must live. We must

keep moving. We are slow. We no longer have the long stride of the horse to help us. We can no longer gallop on its back or warm ourselves with its breath.

He felt a pain in his heart as again the memory of the animal resurfaced.

Then, all of a sudden, he was struck by a thought. Did the child have to survive? Would it really make any difference if she did?

The thoughts emerged like a fish rising to the surface of the water to eat an insect. Unexpected, quick, energetic.

The Hero turned his yellow eyes to the child, who was following him wrapped in the fur. She lagged behind and he stopped to wait for her. Hansio's expression became grave and accusatory. His hand smoothed the stallion's mane.

The girl had her large eyes fixed on the boggy ground, the snow now only appearing in sporadic patches.

Hansio noticed she was short of breath. He had forgotten how vile and suffocating the air of the Infested Lands could be. His lungs were used to it, but the girl's? Even he was feeling more breathless than usual.

It is not just the wounds—we have gone too deep into these lands for too long, he mused.

The girl caught up with him and lifted her chin to the sky. Hansio took a long deep breath and she did the same. The failing sun was now at the highest point in the sky.

Hansio decided they should stop for a rest and slid his sack down the length of his sword. It hit the mud with a watery splash.

The Hero was still gazing at the sky, seeking the comfort that the sun always seemed to give him, when he felt the little girl's hand tighten around his index finger.

He frowned and looked down. His hand was on the hilt of the sword and the child was trying to stop him nervously smoothing the lock of mane he kept there.

She drew her hand away abruptly and he laid the sword on
the ground and sat down on a small dead tree trunk.
His shoulders were slumped over, legs bent and slightly
apart, his elbows leaning on his knees, hands dangling
between them. He bowed his head to avoid the girl's
undecipherable gaze.
He heard her tiny feet sink into a muddy puddle. She was
about to sit down on the trunk beside him, next to the sword.
Hansio tilted his head just enough to glimpse what the child
was doing. She had gripped the hilt of the sword and,
although she was not strong enough to lift the entire weapon,
she had managed to lean the hilt on the trunk. Without
undoing the knot that bound the lock of hair, her tiny fingers
untied the leather lace that attached it to the sword. The fur
slipped off her shoulders, but the cold did not seem to bother
her.
The child cupped the lock of hair in her palms, as if trying to
hold water. Then she joined her hands together and brought
them to her mouth.
Surprised, Hansio watched intently.
The little girl blew into her hands then opened them again. It
looked as if she was playing, but something prevented
Hansio from stopping her.
She took the lock between two fingers and held it in front of
her slanted eyes, before placing it on the trunk between
them. Then, all of a sudden, she shivered and covered herself
with the fur.
The lock was just the same. The child had only blown on it,
as if warming herself with her own breath. Hansio imagined
the stallion had done the same for her, during those dark
hours inside the tomb when he thought he was doomed to
transform into one of the living dead.
They did not look at each other again for a while. When it
was time to set off, Hansio touched her on the shoulder and

she understood, immediately standing and resuming their progress. After a moment, the Hero got to his feet, picked up his sack and sword, but hesitated before taking the lock of mane. He could not explain his hesitation, but as he reached out a hand to take it, tying it to his sword as he had done before, he suddenly felt strange.

He could not believe it, but there was no longer a weight in his breast, even when the gurgling whinny of the horse returned to his mind.

The memory of the animal was but a scar full of affection.

* * * *

Hansio walked carrying the child, who had fallen asleep in his steady arms. They had abandoned the river the day before, because it was now heading towards the Gray Sea, to hurl itself from the rocks and unite with the vast expanse of water. The waterfall lay within the Infested Lands.

The Frontier was near.

As he walked across a moor, dotted with mud and dry bushes, he saw a tree just a hundred paces away. It was tall and leafless and had an intense, opaque, brown color, which stood out amongst the lifeless vegetation around them.

Hansio headed towards it, amazed by its unusual hue. He set the child down at the foot of the tree and she woke. Hansio caressed the slender trunk and branches. He snapped one of its smaller branches, and found the plant was still alive. His gaze turned upwards to the dull, washed-out blue of the sky.

"This plant is still alive," he told the drowsy child. "The Dying Lands are close."

To determine their location, he looked at the sun, whose light shone tepidly, yet almost pleasurably. He scanned the territories to the north, from where they had come, and saw a terrifying panorama. Sinister clouds loomed in the distance and thunderbolts lacerated the sky. This was not the kind of storm Hansio was used to.

To the east he saw a succession of hills that grew taller and taller, losing themselves in the gray mist. There were also hills to the west, lower with gentler peaks. Then he turned his gaze to the south. There, at the foot of two ridges, he saw a tower of the Resistance; one of the outposts built by the Hastur. It was small, very small.

"Maybe you will live, after all," he murmured to the child. "Your secret will be used by the Hastur, whatever it might be. I do not see any magic in you, yet you are not a child like all the others. On this, the sorcerers are right."

The little girl seemed oblivious to any prophecy which concerned her. She yawned and he took her back in his arms. Hansio headed towards the Dying Lands with a lighter heart. The child leaned her head wearily on his shoulder, lulling herself with his decisive steps. Hansio watched as her eyes closed and she returned to her slumber.

Hansio knew he would not reach the Frontier before sunset. Dry bushes, what was once heather, crackled beneath his feet. The air was lighter and his breathing improved—if they were near a river he might even risk drinking the water. It was not clear or clean but it was certainly better than the snow gathered from the bowels of the Infested Lands, or the river water further north.

He was thirsty and hungry—they had finished the Hastur crackers two days ago.

As he watched for signs of life at the tower, a ray of sunlight flickered from the turrets, as it reflected off metal. A helmet perhaps, or a blade.

Soon after, he saw the enormous doorway open and a knight on horseback galloped towards them.

A Hero, he thought, instinctively. Then he corrected himself, remembering.

No, I am the last Hero.

This was reinforced when he noticed that the sword the

knight brandished was not one of those rare specimens from the miraculous forges of the Hastur, but a normal layman's weapon.

Hansio unsheathed his own sword and noticed the light blue glow, common in the Infested Lands.

"He's coming to attack us," he whispered to the child. "He thinks we're living dead."

Hansio knew the warriors of the Frontier, even those from the towered outposts, poorly armed and equipped, were people who struck first and reasoned later.

As the knight drew closer he saw he wore chainmail, rather than the more commonly-used armor. The metal reflected a red ray of sunset. Hansio momentarily forgot the knight and lost himself in thought, hypnotized by the warm light.

I am alive and I shouldn't be, he mused. My horse is dead, yet I suffer no more.

Before his distracting thoughts took over, his Hero instincts kicked in once again.

He easily deflected the first violent blow and swiftly caught the knight by his arm, unsaddling him. The knight lost his weapon and rolled across the ground, leaving a trail in the soft earth. Hansio pounced upon him. Placing one foot on his neck, he pointed the Hastur sword at his would-be assailant. He spoke, moved by a proud impulse that had been dormant for a long time.

"Do you see this blade?" he demanded. "Do you know the magic that makes it glow with a blue light?"

* * * *

Hansio rose to the top of the small tower and peered to the west. It was night.

Every tower of the Resistance had a large mirror and a tar-covered pyre, ready to burn in the event of danger. He had forgotten. Behind him the light of a small fire reflected off the mirror to the east.

To the west, a few leagues away, he recognized a flickering luminous dot. It was far too low in the sky to be a star.

The other sentinel is alive, he thought.

Then he turned towards the small fire that warmed his back. "If this light went out, it would mean the soldier of the tower was dead."

When he still felt like a Hero, the patrols were much more numerous and the tower outposts were not guarded by just one warrior. Communication often occurred by word of mouth, when they met at the confines of their respective territories. Hansio shook his head, discouraged and incredulous.

The sentinel he had unhorsed offered them food and water. They remained protected by the thick walls of the outpost for just one night. They slept in the stable but, even though he found himself in the safest place he had been for many days, Hansio still watched over the child all the time. The night passed peacefully.

* * * *

The soldier stood in silence. As he watched them leave the following morning, he murmured, "I did not know there were any Heroes left. The death of Martos caused great alarm. Many fled to the south."

Hansio silenced him with one look of his sharp, yellow eyes. Hansio took food and drinking water with him, but decided against taking one of the sentinel's horses. Of the two, only one was in good health and the sentinel would need it. This was not the real reason for his decision. He no longer suffered at the thought of the death of his steed, but a sense of caution or mournful respect made him feel sick at the thought of being on another horse.

If a companion-in-arms died in battle, nothing and no one could ever replace them. Certainly, one day, he would choose another, but this mission had started and continued thanks to him, and it would end in his memory.

The release from the oath would signify freedom for both of us, he thought as he continued on his way.

They travelled slowly but with the certainty they would pass through much safer places before reaching the nearest village. Although it was a two-day journey from the tower, this would be the first settlement on the road to the distant Hastur Tower. That was where he would deliver the girl.

* * * *

The inhabitants of the village were exhausted by the air of putrefaction that emanated from the Infested Lands. Yet Hansio was surprised at how the ground he walked on seemed less acidic, so much so they were able to grow food in small allotments, which he caught sight of behind some of the houses. Even more extraordinary was the fact that the air smelt much lighter in some parts of the village. It brought to mind a memory from his childhood. He was on the edge of some rocks by the Gray Sea and the sky was unusually clear, just like the one he looked at now. The wind blew through his hair and made his eyes water. In all his life, he never breathed such pure air. Would he again? It was a memory he now cherished.

With his head still turned to the sky in search of the sun, he was moved again by a now-familiar conundrum. It was the same surprising sensation he felt on top of the tomb, shortly after waking but this time he looked at it differently. It was no longer a merciless torturer that kept an agonized world alive, but a benevolent entity giving humanity its last rays of warmth and light. Even Hansio felt different inside.

He lowered his gaze and looked at his hands. I did not become living dead? Why? I was definitely bitten...

He stopped in the street and the child played listlessly with a stone, as if waiting for the Hero to come back to his senses. Hansio noticed an old man staring at him, his eyes passing ravenously from him to the child. Suddenly someone let out a cry and, when he turned, he noticed a man and woman talking animatedly as they headed towards a square partially hidden behind a house. Other people scurried in the same direction carrying baskets and water bags.

"We will find a tavern later. Now I want to see where those people are going," he told the child, gathering her in his arms.

On his short walk he passed a house, struck by a ray of sun. It was painted a faded crimson, but that color shone. He passed another one that had a creamy yellow hue and a pang of hunger wrenched through his stomach. The sight of the dwellings suddenly made him realize how hungry he was.

As they got closer, the voices grew louder and Hansio heard people praying in chorus. A family—a father, mother, grandfather and newborn son—rushed past them.

When he finally arrived at the square he found it much more crowded than he anticipated. Some prayed in a circle, others moved inwards, their sacks brimming with water. Others jostled and shouted, selfishly pushing the weaker ones aside. It was a long time since he saw so many people in one place. So many living people, that is. It seemed strange to him how such a small village, so close to the Frontier, could be home to so many.

Hansio was much taller than nearly all of them, but still could not see what attracted everyone's attention. Something was happening in the middle of the square.

With the child in his arms, he climbed up a flight of steps that led to the doorway of a house and propped his saddlebag between his feet. As his back touched the wooden door it moved slightly and the hinge gave way. The house, like many others in the square, was abandoned. Hansio took a step backwards into the doorway and finally saw the reason for all the commotion.

There, in the square, were two Hastur.

Anger filled him when he recognized their tunics, but this was soon replaced by amazement when he realized what they were doing.

The first distributed something—food possibly. The other dealt with various people holding out water sacks, canteens and buckets full of water. The second Hastur was blessing the people who crowded around him, conducting some sort of ceremony. Straining to get a better view, he saw the religious man take a white powder from a large sack by his side and pour it into the water. When he finished, he muttered a few words and stirred the liquid with a wooden stick. After he completed his work, Hansio watched as the people became filled with gratitude and enthusiasm. They kissed the Hastur's feet and lavished him with bows. Hansio paid particular attention to one of the poor souls. He watched him leave the crowd and bend down by a child to give him a drink, filling his son's mouth with the treated water.

Hansio was astonished. The Hastur has made the foul water drinkable with his magic, he thought.

They do care about the people. They do care about life after all.

He searched again for the Hastur among the crowds. When he found him he felt a lance through his heart.

The Hastur stared directly at him.

Hansio had been seen and it disturbed him. He immediately searched for an escape route but the Hastur turned away and returned to tending to the people.

* * * *

They found an inn and Hansio asked for a hot bath for the child and some clothes that would fit her. The innkeeper and his wife donated some clothes which belonged to their son, who had died the year before.

Hansio put the child to bed and looked out of the window of the small room. He took his pipe and smoked what was left of the few leaves that remained intact during his journey. For the first time he finally felt he could indulge himself. He could finally permit himself some time to numb his mind with the effects of the smoke.

The pain disappeared. His thoughts became mellower, less angry.

Chapter Thirteen

Hansio stood on a small hill. The lands that opened out before him levelled as they neared the horizon. It was from here that a place known as the Green Plain began. From his position, Hansio saw for many leagues in all directions, even as far as the Hastur Tower. The Tower was a blue glare far in the distance visible even in the bright light of day.

They climbed down the hill and continued across the plain. It would take them at least a day of steady walking to reach their destination.

As they approached, the Tower became more recognizable. As soon as they set foot on the Green Plain it became a luminous ray that united the sky and earth, a needle tasked with holding up the sky, to stop it crashing to earth.

Hansio had made his oath in that place built of stone and magic.

He had never seen the Ark. No Hero had ever set eyes upon it, but it was said to be in that tower. No one had ever been allowed to see it. The Hastur used it as an act of faith. Over the centuries, many tried to give it a form, and not just the artists, but it was merely conjecture and the work of imagination. The religious leaders wanted people to talk about it, preaching of its importance for the human race and for this reason they preferred to rely on the power of popular imagination. However, they never gave precise details. So vague were they, that Hansio always suspected it was only accessible to a small number of Hastur—the Higher Hastur.

He saw many people praying in the village square and he recognized some of their prayers. In them, the Ark became a symbol of hope. It was much more than a mere icon while they waited for the day of the Great Exodus. Some even claimed it was not a physical object like a ship or a chariot, but instead a magic formula or a chant that would lead

humanity to salvation. A chant which, until that time, the
Hastur had been unable to decipher from the divine words.
The language of the gods is not for the ears of men.
It was one of the first doctrines Hansio of the Gray Sea
accepted when he became a Hero.

* * * *

"That tower is where we are going," Hansio told the child.
"Once we are there, I will entrust you to the Hastur and I will
be released from my oath. I will be free."
Hansio took the little girl's hand in his and in that same
instant she tripped on a stone. The shoes they had been
given were far too big for her, but it was still better than
being naked under a fur drenched in the smell of death. She
still clutched the rag doll, which dragged across the ground.
The Hero felt the child's fingers agitating in his palm. They
wriggled as if she wanted to free herself from his grasp.
Without realizing, he suddenly became aware he was
crushing her hand. After a moment of hesitation, he finally
let go. Distracted by his own thoughts he forgot to apologize.
I was hurting her. I thought of leaving her and she refused
my hand.
Inside the masculine clothes, the child had still not lost the
sense of innocence and fragility she always had. On the
contrary, in that very moment, she appeared even more like
a creature estranged from reality.
Hansio had never stopped being struck by her large, slanting
eyes, that excessively slender body, those arms that were a
bit too long, her muteness and all the other little things that
made her strange or maybe even exceptional, considering the
Hasturs' interest in her. Every time he looked at her, it was
as if he saw all those traits for the first time.
"Are you the reason why everyone prays?" Hansio spoke the
question aloud, despite knowing he would never get an
answer.

He smoothed the lock of the horse's mane—something he had not done since the day she touched it. They continued side by side without another word.

Hansio's thoughts shifted and he considered how the Green Plain had no reason to be given that name. In fact, its colors were that of the severest autumn, brown, dirty yellow, dark red. The name must surely have an extremely ancient origin. He raised his yellow eyes and looked for the sun. It was warm and brighter than usual.

* * * *

The Hastur Tower was an extremely tall and imposing structure. Its contours could be distinguished from almost a league away. The blue ray came from the center and touched the sky, but the entire structure emitted streaks of blue light. As a child, he was told the tower in the Green Plain was not the only one in existence. In ancient times, similar structures were erected in the north, but later devoured by the Infested Lands, hundreds, maybe even a thousand leagues beyond the present Frontier. It was a legend, but the Hastur never denied it.

The people always said they were building a new tower farther south. They took it for granted this too would eventually be swallowed up.

Hansio had never been to the Southern Lands. His life unfolded along the broken ribs of the Gray Sea, and, later, along the Frontier or beyond. Sooner or later the land will die and even the Hastur will have to acknowledge it, he thought bitterly.

Hansio took the child in his arms and quickened his pace. He wanted to reach their destination as quickly as possible. They finally arrived at the tower and he stood there contemplating it, suddenly realizing how lost he felt. He could not remember if he had been aware of its majesty or had felt such an emotion on the day of his oath.

It could not be the work of human hands, or rather, not only.
The tower had a circular base, built from blocks of stone each
the size of three horses. They leaned against each other so
precisely that they gave the impression the tower was built
from a single block of stone. The gaps were so small he
thought they must have been made using some form of
magic. Despite this, from close up, Hansio saw the blue glow
seeping out through the fissures from the inside.
The Hero could have sworn not even water could filter
between those blocks of stone.
Hansio put the girl down and took her hand. He knew he was
holding it too tightly and that he might hurt her, but a feeling
of alarm, which he could not explain, had gripped his heart.
His protective instinct was still very strong.
They presented themselves before the mighty door made of
dark, shiny wood, stopping just twenty paces away.
They were halted by the presence of two disturbing and
majestic statues, taller than twenty men. Their imposing
stature had the power to stop anyone who stood before the
tower door. Hansio of the Gray Sea, the last Hero of the
Dying Lands, was not immune to their effect. Their
suggestiveness made him stop and reflect.
The statues represented two beings in human form. The one
on the right was a warrior, clad in ancient armor, its hand
resting on the hilt of a sword which pointed to the ground.
Protected by a helmet, the head looked down at them
menacingly.
The one to the left, wrapped in a cape, held its hands to the
sky as if searching for the sun. Despite their different poses,
both sculpted faces had an unworldly severity. They were
cold and immobile, but they looked as if they would suddenly
speak or move. Hansio wondered if they were a portrayal of
Hastur men or gods in human form. All he knew was they
represented life in this dying world and life after the Great

Exodus.

Maybe they are right. Maybe the child will take us far away from this dying sun.

The girl was beside him. He felt her presence— her life force. He felt life run through his body as fluid— as blood. He still squeezed her hand but, unlike before, he had the impression the child found reassurance in his painful grip. Somehow, that painful bond protected her.

It brought to mind the image of a trembling leaf on a dead branch, at the mercy of a furious wind.

In that moment he realized everything the sun in the sky had ever inspired in him could also be found in the slender form of the child at his feet. Hansio waited no longer.

It was difficult to imagine the people hidden behind these statues and walls were the same compassionate beings he saw in the village.

They took a few steps forward and as soon as they passed between the two statues the immense portal opened. They were suddenly cloaked by the blue light from within. There was silence, and they were alone. Hansio could not hear the sound of mechanical cogs and, as they crossed the threshold, there was no one to be seen, no shadows darting against the light.

Magic alone opened that door and without anyone announcing their arrival.

They continued as best they could, blinded by the intense blue light.

Hansio could not see beyond the portal and the memories of the day of his oath vanished from his mind. He heard the door close behind them and found himself engulfed by the blue glow. He drew the child closer. Hansio did not know what to do. One hand gripped the child, the other instinctively touched the hilt of his sword. There was no apparent reason to be afraid, but something in his heart made him distrust the Hastur.

Once he respected them, then he hated them. Now, he was no longer sure.

All of a sudden, a whispering voice pronounced his name. Both Hansio and the child turned to the right.

"Hero," it whispered again.

Hansio looked at the child, who still had the same lost expression. He longed to know what she was thinking.

"Hansio of the Gray Sea," the voice called.

Hansio followed the sound as it repeated over and over again. He followed blindly, not knowing where they were going. The unbearably uniform blue light was everywhere. It was as if they were back in the darkness of the circular hall beneath the Valley of Tombs.

"Hansio, stop!" the whispering voice ordered, in a tone which was authoritative but gentle.

The blue light dissolved like mist and the scene Hansio found before him was beyond the limits of his human comprehension. There was no sign of the halls he had seen on the day of his oath.

It seemed as though a human foot had never stepped on that marble floor, and it shone like glass.

There were no drapes on the walls, no religious symbols, no banners of any Heroes, no emblems of a noble warrior line. There were not even any walls encircling the hall, which seemed to be infinite. The smell of meadows, moistened by the morning dew, filled the air. It was so intense it could have eliminated the smell of death throughout the Dying Lands.

Above him was the sky as he had never seen it before. He doubted it was the sky of his own world. This begged an important question. What other world could it be?

He doubted a place of this kind, without walls and with such a potent fragrance, could even exist.

Yet...Hansio's feet stood firmly on that marble floor.

Above his head a blue sky was crossed by billowing white clouds. The fresh air which filled his lungs was invigorating. All these things felt palpable and real.

A series of columns, the summits of which vanished out of sight, helped give perspective and dimension, without which Hansio would have lost all reason. He would have found it impossible to recognize left from right, above from below. He felt the consistency of the floor but the marble's veins resembled streams of vapor. It was as if they walked on a thin layer of glass, magically held up by smoke. Wavering smoke inside an unnatural void, he thought.

Hansio was astonished. It was an infinite place. Could their magic really extend to this?

His clutch on the girl's hand helped to keep him sane. The heartbeat he felt under his fingertips kept his legs steady. Without her beside him, he felt he would have lost his sanity—an unsettling thought for a Hero.

Was he the child's protector or was she protecting him?

A human form appeared as if from nowhere. The figure walked towards them with slow, measured steps. The contours gradually became clearer and presently an old, naked man, with a perfectly intact body despite his advanced years, stood before them.

When he was finally clearly in view, a backdrop appeared behind him that left Hansio speechless.

Other men appeared in the distance, naked and focused upon him and the child.

The Higher Hastur, he thought. Clothes are unnecessary when you live in the eyes of the gods.

To the left, a large circle of square-shaped stones penetrated into the marble. The monoliths were immense and from within the circle came the most potent ray of blue light he ever saw. This had to be the work of the most powerful

Hastur magic. It soared into the sky and Hansio realized they were in the center of the tower. The luminous ray was the same one that shone out beyond the peak of the tower, the one that could be admired from many leagues away.

One of the Higher Hastur came to meet them, standing just a few steps away. His face was furrowed by the years and covered in a thick beard. His hair was long and white and grew all the way down to the ground. Hansio followed its natural movement and noticed the tips did not touch the marble but went beyond it, penetrating the surface into the smoky void beneath.

"Hansio of the Gray Sea," the Hastur said. "Do not try to understand what you see. Live, that is all." The voice sounded like vibrating crystals.

Hansio's yellow eyes fixed on his face.

"Where are we?" he asked.

"This place was built following the voices of the gods. What you see below is the Ark. You are the first Hero to have had such a privilege."

Hansio could not believe his ears. The Ark. It really did exist.

"You have accomplished your mission, last Hero of the Dying Lands."

"This is the child." Hansio spoke the words without leaving her side.

"You risked your life," the Hastur acknowledged, warily pointing at the wound on his neck.

"I survived the bite of a Hooded One." Hansio nodded. "I have no idea why."

The news caused the Hastur to become grave and he stared at the child with a scowl.

"Maybe you, the Hastur, can give me an answer."

The Higher Hastur, met Hansio's gaze, his expression still severe.

"What you have said is impossible. Are you certain you were

bitten? It could have wounded you some other way."
Hansio sensed the hostility in his words— the scowl on the Hastur's face remained the same.
"I am not mistaken."
"From the shape and position, it looks as though you were attacked from behind," the Hastur observed.
"In fact, that was how it occurred," Hansio replied unflinchingly. "I saw my own flesh dangling between its teeth."
Hansio noticed a subtle change in the Hastur's expression and realized he would have to content himself with the answer he had been given.
Meanwhile, two of the Higher Hastur detached themselves from the group and approached them.
"The gods say only those who possess a pure and great soul can be saved from damnation. Hansio of the Gray Sea, do you possess such a soul?"
"The soul does not..." Hansio began. Then he stopped himself. He did not have the inner strength to oppose them by declaring he did not believe in the soul. As his mind fleetingly returned to the dead body of his wife, he was pervaded by an overwhelming feeling of anger.
The Hastur had stopped looking at him, his attention now on the child. Hansio noticed another two Hastur, who had stopped and were waiting behind him.
The religious man in front of him was immobile yet beseeching, as if calling the child towards him, an uncanny, false smile on his face.
Hansio did not release his grip and neither did the child make any attempt to move forward. He had not forgotten why he came.
"First," he said, "I want to be freed from my oath."
The Hastur did not even glance in his direction before replying.

"Unsheathe the sword that was given to you and abandon it on this sacred soil, Hansio of the Gray Sea. Then you will be released from your oath, but your irises, the color of a ray of sun, will remain forever."

"As long as I still have sight, I do not care what color my eyes are."

Hansio let go of the child's hand, unsheathed his sword and gripped it in both hands. With the tip pointing to the ground, he plunged it into the shiny marble at his feet. It was a gesture which was both furious and liberating.

The enchanted place echoed with the jarring sound of his gesture, like a blade against glass. However, it was followed by something unexpected. His muscles were still swollen, his arms tense, his hands still clutching the hilt of the sword, when the child suddenly clung onto him. She gripped the top of his arm, leaning her cheek against it.

"You are free, you are discharged. Nothing more will be asked of you. Now give us the child," the Hastur urged when he saw the girl's reaction.

Hansio bent down and gently held her chin between his fingers. The sight of those large eyes in that innocent face caused a stabbing pain in his stomach.

"Do not be afraid," Hansio whispered to the child. "Remember the men who were doing good deeds in the village? The ones who were giving out bread and purifying the water? These are the same men. You will be safe here." He bent down slowly and kissed her forehead.

The child responded by holding his head in her hands and bringing her lips close to his. Their skin touched and the child blew gently into his mouth. Hansio felt her breath move through his lungs. The significance of the gesture, which felt oddly poignant, was lost on him. There was still so little about the child he understood.

He released the child from his grasp and got back up on his

feet.

Momentarily, he felt a sense of regret, but now he had what he deserved, he was free.

Still, questions haunted him. Did the child have a soul? he wondered, desperately.

She left his side and took the hand of the Hastur, who still hid behind his smile, which he wore like a mask.

She will be safe with them, he told himself. Maybe the child really does have a great soul and maybe she is the one who will save the human race.

The two Hastur waiting nearby took the child's hand and walked away, turning their backs on him.

The Hastur who spoke, however, turned once more to Hansio.

His expression changed as the smile transformed into something more severe and cold.

"Go!" the Hastur boomed. "You are no longer welcome here. You have already seen more than you should. Return to your deplorable life. Return to your belief that the soul does not exist."

The soul, the soul, the soul.

"Wait. I can't hear anything at all," said Hansio impulsively, suddenly aware of the gnawing silence in the tower. "Where are the voices of the gods?"

The Hastur did not reply.

Hansio was suddenly engulfed in a blue light and the background became blurred and uniformly bright. The child, the Hastur and the Ark vanished.

His mind repeated the same mantra, the soul, the soul, the soul.

Something still disturbed him. Why did his thoughts keep returning to the existence of the soul? What was the soul? Why did the gods say that only those with a great soul deserved to be saved?

He resigned himself to never getting a satisfactory answer. From that moment onwards he was a free man, even free from the obligation to believe in the soul. Free to give importance to human life in the manner he saw fit.

He cast a last glance towards the sword in the marble floor, the last object he was able to see, before it was swallowed by the blue light. The lock of the stallion's mane was still tied to the cross-shaped hand-guard. He stood motionless. He could have stepped forward and taken it—he could have done. Yet, he was paralyzed by his thoughts.

An idea struck him like an epiphany.

Does the child have a soul? he thought.

He hesitated no longer and, driven by instinct, he grabbed the sword.

The blue light cleared as if it were mist sucked up by the breath of a giant monster.

Everything reappeared, the Ark, the Hastur, and the infinite room. Light flickered upon the countless columns and dispersed.

Only one thing had changed.

The rag doll lay on the floor.

Convinced something irreparable had happened, Hansio drew the sword from the marble with improbable force.

The Hastur stood in a circle at the center of the Ark, each one next to a corresponding monolith.

Hansio could not see the child.

Even the Hastur seemed unaware of his presence.

Brandishing the sword, he ran gasping toward the Ark. Even the space was deceptive. Distances were distorted, they stretched and contracted even as he watched.

He arrived near the Ark and what he saw beyond the heads of the Higher Hastur froze the blood in his veins. He slowed his steps and saw the child lying on her back in the exact center of the circle the religious men had formed.

Out of breath and blind with rage, he felt on the precarious brink of madness.

Hansio immediately realized that in this place, time did not seem to follow the rules he knew. For him, only a few seconds had elapsed, but for the Hastur it was obvious a much longer period of time must have passed.

He was devastated, overwhelmed by a turbine of emotions which would have driven lesser mortals insane. His legs trembled and buckled beneath him. The sword clashed against the marble, producing a sound of unnatural quality. He dropped to his knees.

What he saw was horrific.

The child was naked.

The child was dead.

They had ripped out her heart, which now lay above her chest. It was huge—Hansio could have sworn it belonged to a man of his own stature—but there was no doubt it belonged to the child, because her chest was wide open. A piece of drooping flesh hung down from the gaping wound. It looked as though she was sleeping. Her eyes were closed, her eyelids tightly shut. Her thorax had been emptied and the tiny body seemed much more slender than he remembered.

I will never see those eyes open again, thought Hansio.

Not a drop of blood marked the marble around her.

Suddenly there was a subtle shift in the atmosphere. The Hastur knew he was there, Hansio realized, but no one moved and no one spoke.

It seemed an eternity since he handed her over to the Hastur. Hansio scanned their near-identical faces until he recognized the one who freed him from his oath. In that moment, of all the feelings that had washed over him, only anger remained. Using his sword for support he rose to his feet and walked towards him. Each step was heavy, strenuous, painful.

Fixing him with a steady gaze, Hansio asked, "Where are the

voices of the gods?"

The Hastur replied calmly, as if suddenly freed from a grave responsibility. "The gods have not spoken with us for a thousand years."

Hansio kept his voice calm, trying to contain the fury burning underneath.

"Is this the reason I cannot hear their voices?"

"You cannot hear them because they no longer speak," the Hastur said.

"The child gave me her soul." Hansio spoke slowly, acknowledging what must surely be the truth. "That is why I'm still alive. That is why I did not transform."

"Precisely." The Hastur confirmed his fear in a single word.

"So, why did you tear out her heart?" Hansio cried, incredulous. "She could have helped us. She was important for the Ark."

Hansio gripped the sword tightly and his muscles quivered. Not even the living dead had caused him so much fury.

"Because she had to die," came the answer.

Hansio exploded and raised his sword. The Hastur stretched out a hand, as if that gesture was all it would take to placate the Hero's wrath. It could not dowse the flames. Hansio's powerful thrust cut off the entire limb and forced the sword into the solid marble. The arm fell to the ground, shattering into a thousand pieces, as if it were made of crystal.

"Hacking me to pieces will change nothing," the Hastur warned, unmoved.

"It will calm my anger," replied Hansio. "Answer me! Why did you kill her? She was important. She was the most important human being I have ever met. She was the only one with a soul in this soulless world."

The Hastur was not bleeding and did not seem to feel any pain. Even the flesh and bone he had exposed looked as if they were made of glass.

None of the Hastur reacted.

"You said two things," the Hastur replied. "One was right, the other wrong. The child had a soul and she was the only one in this world who possessed one. You are wrong if you think she was human."

Gripped by hate, Hansio let out another anguished cry. He dislodged the sword and slashed at the Hastur's other arm. It fell like the first, breaking in the same way. The sound of the echoing fragments rang through the infinite space long after the arm had disintegrated on the ground.

The Hastur was this time thrown backwards and fell. Again he spoke. "The child was entrusted to a human family. She was kidnapped then saved by you. She had to stay as far away as possible from the Ark and its power, so she would not be influenced by it."

"I will show no mercy, so spare me your false tales, sorcerer."

"The Hastur never lie," he continued, still sprawled on the floor. "The gods stopped speaking to us many centuries ago, when the sun first started to die. Since then we have had to use our knowledge to save humankind."

"The gods do not exist," Hansio insisted. "The soul does not exist."

"The gods did exist," the Hastur said. "Then they disappeared, as I told you before. The Hastur believe in the sacredness of life and we have kept this secret hidden for a thousand years. If not, it would have been the end of everything. In this way, we have given hope. We have given life."

Hansio snorted. "You have prolonged the agony and deceived the poor people who have been slowly devoured by the living dead."

He raised his sword again. "Answer me clearly, why did you kill the child?"

Hansio did not strike, but waited for an answer.

"The reason is the living dead. The child risked becoming a monster like them, if not worse. She was mutating."

Hansio could not believe his ears. This was too absurd, even for a lie.

"The gods stopped talking to us and since that day no one has been born with a soul. Before the silence, however, they taught us how to travel between realities, how to find a new world. They taught us how to use the Ark. Their language is not always easy to comprehend and our search for a suitable world has become endless."

Hansio lowered his sword slightly, pointing it close to the Hastur, who was still on the floor.

"We have visited many places that are inhabited by creatures who, unlike us, still have a soul. With these the gods still speak. This was in a time before I was born, but history tells us that there were countless attempts and many bitter disappointments."

The armless body tried to get up.

"The child was taken from one of these worlds and used to test if our realities might be compatible. There were, and are, too few of us on this world to do anything less. Our lives are too important to allow for experimentation but alien beings can be sacrificed. When we realized this too would be a failure, we did what we had to do, we sent Martos to find her. It is only with her blood that we can close the doorway the Ark created with her world and continue our search elsewhere. The rest you know all too well."

"This makes no sense, sorcerer, this makes no sense," Hansio whispered. "The child saved me, and she gave me her soul. She could do it for the others." His voice was as thin and flimsy as a thread.

"Something of this kind has already happened and it was an unforgiveable mistake."

Despite his desperation, Hansio's mind fixed on a sudden

lucid thought. It became clear what the Hastur was saying.
"So the living dead, the Hooded Ones?"

"Yes," the Hastur confirmed. "Many centuries ago, the Hooded Ones were not as they are now. They came from another world and deceived my predecessors. In the beginning it seemed as though we had found the place for our Great Exodus, but something happened which rendered us powerless."

"They became what they are now..." Hansio breathed.

"Unfortunately, yes. They changed nature, they ran away from the light and our pale sun helped them breed. They devour our flesh. The first they ever tasted was that of a Hastur. Soon, even the half-eaten dead left their tombs and—"

"There is no need for you to say anymore," Hansio cut him off.

He stood up, raised his sword and dropped the blade on the Hastur without pity, splitting his head in two. The other Hastur did nothing to stop him.

An infinite burst of brightly colored crystals scattered, sliding across the marble floor.

Hansio trampled the remains of the Hastur and turned his back.

He did not want to see the body of the child any more. He did not even pick up the doll.

His yellow eyes were empty, no longer filled with rage and hate.

He felt at peace, knowing he had always been right. Now he understood and cursed his desire to seek the truth.

Chapter Fourteen

Hansio walked along the edge of a ravine.

The Hastur sword glowed bright blue. He acknowledged it only fleetingly. The living dead were close by. The lock of the stallion's mane was still tied to the hilt.

A rope was tied around his wrist and stretched out over his shoulder. A few steps behind him a man with a bruised face wailed like a child. He feared for his life.

Hansio dragged him down a steep footpath until they arrived at the bottom of the ravine.

Nearby, a stake had been hammered into the ground, the muddy soil around it soaked with coagulated blood.

The air carried the familiar smell of death and putrefaction common to the Infested Lands.

Hansio's mind was deranged yet eerily calm. Over and over, his thoughts repeated, I have a soul, yet the world around me is soulless.

Bleakly, he returned to his task.

"There is no ultimate certitude that steers us through life," he said.

This was his last good-bye to each and every one of his bait.

ABOUT THE AUTHOR

Alberto Büchi was born in Milan, Italy, in 1978 and graduated in Economics in 2002. Few months later he moved to London to attend the New York Film Academy's European branch, where he experienced the basics of cinematography and narrative techniques. After that he began to work as a filmmaker.

The passion for writing was parallel and constant, especially in his preference for the fantasy and horror genres; the short story "Eleonora," which belongs to the horror genre, won a 2013 competition. It was banned from the site www.TheFear.it. In the same year, he published online some reviews of novels of the same genre, he wrote a book as a ghost-writer, and then began writing "Frontier Wanderer."

Visit him online at: http://www.albertobuchi.com

www.ingramcontent.com/pod-product-compliance
Lightning Source LLC
Chambersburg PA
CBHW072241190626
46809CB00018B/2861